The Reincarnation of Clara

Selected Books by Kevin J. Todeschi

Non-Fiction:

Dream Images and Symbols
Edgar Cayce's ESP
Edgar Cayce on the Akashic Records
Edgar Cayce on Reincarnation and Family Karma
Edgar Cayce on Soul Mates
Edgar Cayce on the Book of Revelation
Edgar Cayce's Twelve Lessons in Personal Spirituality
God in Real Life

Fiction:

A Persian Tale
The Reincarnation of Clara
The Rest of the Noah Story

The Reincarnation of Clara

By Kevin J. Todeschi

Yazdan Publishing
Virginia Beach • Virginia

Copyright 2011
By Kevin J. Todeschi

Printed in the U.S.A.

All rights reserved. No part of this book may be used or reproduced in any manner whatsoever without written permission except in the case of brief quotations embodied in critical articles of reviews.

Yazdan Publishing
P.O. Box 4604
Virginia Beach, VA 23454

ISBN 13: 978-0-9845672-4-9

Cover design by Richard Boyle

Text and design layout by Cathy Merchand

"I want very much to tell my story. I think many people could learn something from my life ... you see, there are 'patterns' that have become so clear to me. Patterns that go back way before I was ever even born. There may not be another story like this in all the world."

Clara Cabot, in the summer of her 85th year

One

HUNTSVILLE, UTAH— SUMMER MORNING, 2006

A slight breeze circulated the air around the porch but it was hot and dry, and in spite of the proximity of the Great Salt Lake, there was no moisture anywhere to be found. The few tomato plants Clara Cabot had found time to plant that year appeared straggly and neglected but instead of rising to address the situation, Clara simply shook her head, turned toward the driveway, and continued rocking. At 85, it was sometimes hard to find the energy to do much of anything. Besides, she wanted to save her strength for the interview. At long last, it was time to tell the story.

She rocked back and forth on her big, white Victorian porch and waited. The porch table had been laid out with a pitcher of lemonade, two glasses, and a small plate of those chocolate mint covered Oreos that Clara saved for special occasions. A very worn map of the state of Idaho had also been set on the table. On the porch next to her rocker, Clara had placed a very large hatbox.

There wasn't any need to look at her watch—Clara knew how soon the woman was coming. She had known when the interview would take place a very long time before even the paper or the reporter had known. That's just the way it was with Clara—she seemed to know things way ahead of everybody else. Her late husband, Joe, had loved that about her. He had loved the fact that she could look back on the past with considerable skill, as well.

From where she sat, she could see the large signs "Huntsville Air Force Base" and "Government Property: No Trespassing" on the enormous chain-link fence that stood just beyond her property line. The base was nearly abandoned now as a result of U.S. military base shutdowns. There had been a time, however, when the noise of jet engines had been as common as the rustling of tree branches that now came to her ears.

"That damn noise nearly drove me crazy!" Clara reflected aloud.

Just then the Toyota pulled into her driveway; Clara rose and stood, waiting for the reporter, her niece, to come to her.

"At long last, it's time," the old woman whispered to herself.

As Joan got out of the car, it was obvious that the thirty-something woman was at least eight months pregnant. Clara had known that Joan was expecting, but hadn't considered the possibility that the birth might take place right in the middle of her interview. She thought about it for a moment and then shook her head to the contrary, "Eleven days to go," Clara spoke with certainty, although it was well before her niece was within earshot.

With some measure of difficulty, Joan lugged a large bag with the logo and header of the "Salt Lake Tribune" emblazoned on one side. The woman's name: Joan E. Stuart, appeared as script lettering in the lower right. When Clara saw the script, she was reminded that she had seen her niece's name in the paper many more times than she had actually seen the woman herself. "These are regrets," Clara whispered, as she pushed the thought from her mind. She stood until her niece climbed to the top of the porch.

"I'm glad you could come, Joanie," Clara extended a hand, and Joan shook it dutifully before Clara sat back in her rocker.

Joan pulled out a small digital tape recorder, a pen, and a writing tablet, and responded just as she placed the bag on the floor. "To tell you the truth, Clara, this is not really my kind of assignment but Martin, my editor, thought he was doing me a favor because of my condition."

"You're also my niece, Joanie."

Joan simply nodded, took her seat, and stated somewhat reluctantly, "Martin thought it might make an interesting Sunday feature, what with you being an eyewitness to this area for sixty years."

"I've outlasted the base. That noise nearly drove me crazy. But this is where I've belonged. You know, Joanie, I've been wanting to get you out here to talk with me for a very long time." When there was no response, Clara added: "I'm glad you're here. I'm sorry that your boyfriend . . . Larry, isn't it? I'm sorry that Larry wasn't interested in marriage and a baby. I'm also sorry I was never as close to you as I was with your folks, but I'm hoping that by working together on this we can have a fresh start."

Joan looked at her watch and replied: "Let's just get on with it, Clara. How do you want to begin?"

"I want very much to tell my story. I think many people could learn something from my life, Joanie; you see, there are 'patterns' that have become so clear to me. Patterns that go back way before I was ever even born. There may not be another story like this in all the world."

"Just tell me how you want to start."

In spite of Joan's obvious disinterest, Clara simply nodded her head, took the map from the table, and unfolded it. When the map was open, she pointed to a small town listed in the southeastern-most portion of Idaho and moved it back in Joan's direction. "Maybe we should start here, at the very beginning, way back even before I got to Huntsville?"

Clara reached across the table and tapped the location again with a long, boney finger: "The story starts here, but you'll no longer find it on any map. There was a place about fifteen miles outside of Malad; it was called Samaria City. That's where I was born.

"For all practical purposes, all traces of that town are gone. You might say that I was born into a world that no longer exists, in a town that has long since disappeared. It was so different then, like living in another century."

Clara took a bite out of one of the Oreos and continued: "Samaria City sprang up where it did because of the Southern Pacific railroad. Along the tracks, land could be had for $4 an acre and so by 1900 a village had sprung up near that station . . . though, in truth, there were less than thirty houses even by the time I decided to come into the world. I think it's important to make the point that people built near railroad tracks for convenience and not because of the beauty of the train going by." She chuckled.

"Papa bought some land on the outskirts of the town—even Samaria City considered us country-folk. By the late 1930s that little city would grow into a community of nearly two hundred homes. It is hard to believe that by 1960 what remained of the city was consolidated into Malad and Samaria City had all but ceased to exist.

"I was born in the log house that my father built. In all, my poor mama would birth seven children but only four of us would grow to adulthood. My father was Everett Stuart, and my mother Mabel. I had a grandfather that I loved dearly.

"When I was born, I had two brothers, Benjamin and your father, Jason—who was so handsome—and a sister Emily. Later on my parents would have Sara. There was also Nathaniel, who came before me, and Michael, who came after, but they both died the same month they were born. It could be a very harsh time to be alive . . .

"Back then it never even occurred to me that I would see Mama and Papa and all the others dead and buried—these just aren't the thoughts of a young girl growing up on a farm in Samaria City."

Joan looked up from her blank writing tablet and sighed. It was obviously going to be a very long interview. As though oblivious to her reaction, Clara continued her narration:

"As I grew up and became a young woman, I had the adventure of watching that small village become a city. We had our own schoolhouse, a beauty parlor, a grocery store, a barber shop, a tailor shop, several garage and service stations, a few restaurants, even a volunteer fire department. For the most part the churches were Mormon, but there was one Baptist church and that's where Mama and Papa belonged. Benjamin used to say that the good Lord had made us all Baptists just so we wouldn't be getting out of line.

"As a family, we were often together at the Baptist church—that was our social life; whenever the doors were open we were there. Mama had the most beautiful voice . . . she just loved to sing.

"My little sister, Sara, and I were just inseparable, which was fine with me because Emily and I never seemed to be able to get along." Clara looked directly at her niece as if to emphasize this second point before continuing:

"Papa was strict with all of us but he seemed the worst with your father. In fact, Jason was more familiar with that woodshed and the switch than all the rest of us put together. You see, your father was quite a looker, and all the girls in Samaria City had a thing for him, which was improper 'cause no Mormon girl should be setting her sights on a Baptist. I think Papa figured Jason would get into girl trouble early on and he was trying to head things off at the pass.

"It was an innocent time but it was a strict time. We were the frontiers' type people. Life was simple but it could be hard. Free time was the exception rather than the rule. There was no such thing as TV. We had chores, and Papa made certain that the rules were followed to the letter. I cleaned the house and mother did the cooking. I did the ironing, the sweeping, the dusting, and I brought flowers in when they were in bloom. Emily and I were always responsible for doing the dishes.

"Emily was a good cook, in spite of herself. She also did the wash and would hang the clothes out on the line, which ran from the corner of the porch to the big oak tree where Papa had made us a swing. I remember Mama used to say, 'nothing looks homier than a line of drying sheets hanging in the sun.'

"I was close to both of my brothers in different ways, but having Emily for an older sister was a real struggle. You never met Emily—she died of lung cancer before you were born. The two of us shared a bedroom, which made being sisters all the more challenging, but I pretended my bed and my side of the room was my own chamber—just as she had hers. We even drew a line across the floor with chalk. She had this doll that I really wanted. Lord, how Emily was attached to that doll. Mama told me I could have a doll just like it when I was older—it had a porcelain face and everything—but by the time I was older I didn't care no never mind about dolls. I wanted it then . . ."

Finally, Joan interrupted, "Clara, it's really your connection to Huntsville that the paper is interested in."

Clara was only slightly frustrated by the interruption. "I know that, Joanie, but some of this story is important to just me and you. You can skip over this part if you want when you write the article for Martin." The old woman nodded, took another bite of Oreo, seemed to recollect her thoughts and then stated, "Now where was I? Oh yes, mostly, I remember all the work we had to tend to back then. There was always something to be washed, or cleaned, or hoed. There was always something that had to be weeded. We grew sweet potatoes and it was a real job making certain that those weeds didn't overtake them. I also had to pick bugs off the potato vines. Every day I had something to do. But it seems to me that even with all those chores, kids back then depended more on their imagination than they do now. At the time, I think my greatest concern seemed to be wondering how to get out of doing those damn dishes . . .

"But it would all pass much too quickly, and eventually three things would happen that would change my life forever: the discovery that I was somehow very different from other children, my meeting Paul Gabriel, and the death of a four-year-old . . . "

Joan looked up from her blank writing tablet and decided the time had come to turn on the recorder.

SAMARIA CITY, IDAHO— STUART FAMILY HOME, EVENING, 1928

"I hate you Emily Ann Stuart," Clara (at seven) said

to her ten-year-old sister. "Why can't I hold Annabelle?"

"Because she's my doll and not yours, that's why! Besides you have your own dolls!" Emily was wearing her nightgown, pacing in front of the dresser mirror, and desperately trying to see some signs of budding womanhood. She moved her hands to pump her small breasts, as if the motion might encourage even the slightest growth. Clara was sitting on her own bed, wearing a matching nightgown that their mother had sewn. She was holding a kitten in her arms, feeding it from a baby bottle. In spite of the kitten, Clara stared toward the beautiful doll on Emily's bed.

"I promise to be careful . . . "

Emily swung around from the mirror, "I said NO!" Her quick motion caused the gas lantern on the dresser to flicker, just as one of the pages from her papers—"my stories," as she was fond of calling them—fluttered to the floor.

Suddenly, Clara glanced toward the door and grimaced. "Mama's coming!" She had just enough time to remove the kitten from her lap, pushing both kitten and bottle under the bed. Her twin bed was on the wall opposing Emily's. A faint chalk line had been drawn on the floor down the center of the room. Emily lifted a brush from the dressing table and pretended to brush her hair, just as the girls' mother opened the door. Mabel Stuart was wearing an apron and appeared nine months pregnant. She looked at each of her daughters with suspicion.

"What have you two been doing?"

"Nothing, Mama," the reply came in unison.

"It's time for lights out. It's a school day tomorrow."

"Yes, Mama."

"Yes, Mama."

Emily made a pretense of pulling the brush through her hair with one final stroke before walking toward her own bed. She pulled back the covers with one hand, while tightly holding Annabelle with the other. After making certain that Clara could see, she kissed the doll on each cheek and then laid it on the edge of her pillow before getting into bed next to it. When both girls were in bed, Mama reached for the lantern to turn off the gas. Suddenly, from under the bed the kitten cried, and Clara frowned.

"Oh, Clara! What have I told you about bringing that barn cat into this house?" With some measure of difficulty, Mabel Stuart got down on her knees and a moment later dragged both the kitten and the bottle out from under her youngest daughter's bed.

"You're not using a bottle to feed that cat!" Mabel Stuart managed to rise from the floor, still shaking her head in disgust.

"I'm sorry, Mama. I was just pretending she was my baby."

"Clara, one day you'll have children of your own, and it's fine to pretend but I don't want the cat in here again. Understand?" She held the bottle under one arm and the kitten by the scruff of its neck. Her free hand moved toward the lantern.

"Yes, Mama."

"Now it's time for bed. You both have to get up early tomorrow."

"Yes, Mama."

"Yes, Mama."

The lights were turned off and the door was closed, leaving the girls in the darkness of their room. After a moment, Emily whispered from her bed:

"How come you always know when Mama's coming, or Papa, or Jason, or Benjamin? You're always right."

"I don't know . . . I just know."

"If she catches you with that cat again you'll be switched."

"She won't catch me."

"The next time you bring that cat inside, I'm gonna tell."

With her voice trembling, Clara began to cry, "I hate you, Emily Ann Stuart . . . "

Emily was unmoved. "I hate you too!"

HUNTSVILLE, UTAH— SUMMER MORNING, 2006

"We wasted so much time, but Emily could be a tough bit of karma for a seven-year-old," Clara said wistfully. "I don't think my childish mind could have fathomed how many eons the two of us had been arguing."

Although Joan still hadn't taken any notes, she had seemed interested in the story; however, Clara's words caused her to respond patronizingly: "You still believe in reincarnation?"

"It is not a belief! It's either a fact or it isn't. Belief has nothing to do with it. Life either works this way or it doesn't. The things I've seen have made me understand that this is simply a matter of fact."

"Okay, Clara." She turned a page in her notebook and wrote 'HUNTSVILLE' in capital letters, underlining the word twice. "Tell me about moving to Huntsville."

Clara nodded and took a sip from the lemonade. "That makes for a fine story. Actually, you know, it was my first day in Huntsville that I saw the present merge with the past with such clarity that I knew for a fact we had all been here before . . . "

The reporter placed her pen on the tablet and simply listened. The look on her face made it clear that she was irritated with the assignment. Seeing that the story was going to be told Clara's way or not at all, Joan simply relented. "Okay, Clara, tell me about it."

Clara nodded, leaned back in the rocking chair and reminisced aloud:

"After I divorced Paul, I took the Southern Pacific down to Ogden and then a cab into Huntsville. I had left Samaria City devastated from that marriage—you know, Joanie, all I ever wanted to be was a wife and a mother. When the marriage didn't work, I had nowhere to go except for of all places Emily's. Imagine! My life had taken such a turn for the worse that the only place I could go to was a sister's I could not stand. It was 1946 and I was twenty-five years old.

"Emily had gone down to Ogden during the War, a couple of years before I made the move. They were hiring seamstresses for all kinds of uniforms, and canvas, and whatnot. She got an apartment here in Huntsville, because it was cheaper. She was quite skilled with a needle and thread and felt like Ogden was a better place to find a man. Unfortunately, what Emily had kind of forgotten was the fact that it was wartime and there wasn't really a man to be found . . . least not under the age of fifty. Besides, most of the men Emily came across were Mormon and Papa had always had his heart set on a Baptist for each of us. By the time I arrived, Emily was twenty-eight and still single, which was a very sad condition for a woman in those days. I'm not one to judge but by the time I got to Huntsville, Emily was desperate for a man. That was the root cause of the biggest problem between us later on."

Joan leaned back in her own chair just as she felt the baby kick. The interview was not going the way she had planned, and finishing before lunch appeared out of the question. However, she was determined to finish the interview in one day, as she sure didn't want to have to make a return trip. The recorder continued taping, Clara continued speaking, and Joan sighed.

"You okay, Joanie? Clara asked, interrupting herself for only a moment. Joan nodded affirmatively, so Clara began again:

"Anyway, I can remember that day as if it was yesterday. I had arrived earlier than expected and Emily was still out. I took a seat in the lobby of her apartment building—it was really the Ambassador Hotel but the hotel also rented out apartments. I was exhausted, and I was depressed. Here I thought my entire life was over and I was all of twenty-five-years-old. Imagine!

"I've told you before how I can 'look sideways' and see things that others just don't see. I've never known exactly how it works but it's like looking beyond the obvious. Have you ever looked into a mirror with another mirror behind you, and you can just keep seeing way off into the distance? It's like looking all the way to infinity. Anyway, it feels a little bit like that.

"That hotel seemed so foreign to a Samaria City girl. I remember sitting there and wondering what had I even been thinking to come in the first place. I was so tired and devastated, that when I felt myself start to look sideways at that big fancy couch in the lobby; well, I was too tired to fight it. I just let it happen."

Clara turned to her niece with a smile, "That was the first day I saw your Uncle Joe."

TWO

HUNTSVILLE, UTAH—MAIN STREET, SUMMER AFTERNOON, 1946

A Black and White cab pulled up alongside the sidewalk, next to a newsstand containing prominent copies of both the *Salt Lake Tribune* and the *Huntsville Gazette.* Twenty-five-year-old Clara appeared depressed and weary as she got out of the cab. For a moment, she stared at the address held in her hand and then looked up toward the storefronts, which were situated just behind the newsstand. Finding her bearings, she walked past several of the buildings toward her destination.

Finally, she came to the Ambassador Hotel and walked inside. Scattered throughout the lobby were a number of plush and worn red velvet furnishings.

Across from the reservation counter, an ornate staircase led to the hotel's upper levels. Clara took a seat in one of the chairs facing a large velvet couch and waited. Emily had told her that she would come straight to the lobby after work.

"What am I doing here?" Clara sighed to herself and then added: "There was nowhere else to go."

Clara was exhausted. She felt emotionally drained from the divorce, and having to leave Paul. It had also been devastating to leave behind the rest of her family, Samaria City, and everything she had known. But there was no way she could have stayed with Paul in the vicinity.

"For several reasons," Clara muttered to herself.

Because she was tired, she propped her head up with one arm resting on the chair. She took a deep breath and looked at the red couch across from her. She felt her eyes start to look sideways at it, but was just too tired to move. The couch began to blur, as though one copy after another started to appear one behind the other. Suddenly, all she could see was a tremendous flash of light.

FORT LARAMIE, WYOMING—BORDELLO ROOM, 1852

As another red velvet couch came into view, the transparent form of twenty-five-year-old Clara Stuart, formerly Mrs. Paul Gabriel, suddenly realized that she was watching the intimacy between two naked figures lying entwined upon the couch. Although looking sideways had enabled her to see "private business" many times previously—such as the time she had looked in on Paul Gabriel while he was standing wearing nothing but his birthday suit in the boys' locker room—she had never before seen anything quite so personal. The woman had her legs wrapped so tightly around the man's naked waist that it appeared she was fearful he would pull out before the time was right. Suddenly, the woman's soft moans caused Clara to blush and she diverted her eyes elsewhere to give the couple some measure of privacy. It became immediately obvious that she was no longer in 1946.

Even though the light sneaking through the drawn drapes suggested it was midday, Clara could see that the room was very different than the one her conscious mind had just left behind. There was no light switch, no light bulbs, and no appearance of anything having to do with electricity. The dresser might have been considered old fashioned, even when Clara had been a child. By the same standard, the lantern appeared old, as well. The dresser had an old mirror behind it, enabling Clara to see her ghostly reflection. The rest of the furnishings were quaint, all wood, and seemed like they were the product of a handyman, rather than a manufacturer. In one corner of the room, a sleeping baby lay quietly in its crib. The couple's clothing had been quickly discarded and thrown next to the bed. The coonskin cap and the hide jacket made it apparent that the man was some kind of a trapper. The woman's dress could only belong to a dancehall girl.

It was immediately obvious to Clara that she was witnessing shadows of the past, and from prior experience with things less dramatic, she knew the couple would never be able to hear her. The thought made her recall Dickens' *Christmas Carol* and she whispered: "These are the shadows of things that were . . . but where and when am I?" And suddenly she knew—Fort Laramie, Wyoming in 1852.

"But why?" Clara whispered again. She had never even heard of a place called Fort Laramie.

Clara turned back to the couple and wondered who they might be. The scene between the two became more intense; the woman moaned with pleasure. As though putting his mind on other matters, the man looked up and stared in Clara's direction. He had several days' growth of whiskers but appeared to be quite handsome. When he was ready, his own movements began to intensify—pushing himself toward the woman and then pulling back almost to the point of withdrawal. Finally, the woman on the couch let her head fall back over the couch's armrest. Clara gasped and held her breath.

Clara was staring at a woman who appeared to be her identical twin. In fact, there could be no doubt—

she *was* staring at herself! With that awareness, Clara Stuart suddenly realized that she had once lived in Wyoming as a dancehall girl, and that her name at the time had been Esther.

HUNTSVILLE, UTAH—SUMMER MORNING, 2006

"Now, Joanie, let me tell you in the hundreds of times I had looked sideways, I had never seen anything quite so, uh . . . stimulating. Maybe the stress had finally gotten to me and I had broken through some kind of a wall that had always been there. I just don't know. As soon as I saw those two on the couch, I knew I could have pulled back to the hotel but I was too caught up in this happening to want to go anywhere else. Maybe I should have been ashamed for the intrusion but I felt such a part of that scene that . . . well, I just felt I belonged."

Throughout the tale, Joan had been leaning forward in her chair, "Who was the man?"

"It was your Uncle Joe, but I hadn't met him yet. At the time of this Fort Laramie business his name had been Russell. As soon as I saw myself that day in Wyoming . . . well, a whole new understanding of the way things worked came into play. My soul had been here before. I didn't question it. I had seen it with my own two eyes. Took me awhile before I mentioned this to anyone else either—you see, I had really been taunted at school for this whole looking sideways business and what I had just seen went way beyond that.

"Anyway, Emily came back to the hotel some time later and I followed her up to the apartment. I had just started my life as a divorced woman and here my sister Emily was still looking for a man.

"She was a beautiful woman, really," Clara looked up at her niece and added, "she had hair the same color as yours. I just wish she could have done something about those damn, thick glasses of hers. You see, Joanie, back then we didn't have contacts."

HUNTSVILLE, UTAH— EMILY'S APARTMENT, 1946

In the hallway outside of Emily Stuart's apartment, twenty-eight-year-old Emily struggled with her keys before finally getting the door to unlock: "It only works if you twist it back and forth just so."

When the door opened, Emily ushered Clara inside the apartment, pulling her by the arm toward the couch. The apartment was sparsely furnished, although the presence of curtains on the windows and doilies on several table tops displayed Emily's sewing skill. Her Bernina machine was also against one wall, scattered with half-sewn articles that had apparently been brought home from work. As Clara looked around the room, she nodded when she saw

Annabelle, Emily's old doll, propped up in one of the chairs.

Emily took her sister's handbag, placed it on the coffee table and pulled Clara to the sofa, forcing her to take a seat. The table was scattered with pieces of paper that Emily had been writing on, and next to the papers a dirty ashtray appeared three-quarters full.

Clara was shocked, "You've taken up smoking! Mama's gonna be fit to be tied!"

"Never mind about that. I met a man!" Emily reached toward an end table and lifted a newspaper, which had obviously been read and refolded. She held it tightly between her hands.

"Where?" Clara appeared dubious.

"He just moved into the hotel. He's some kind of a top dog for Southern Pacific."

"What do you know about him?"

"He walks with a cane—I think he must have some kind of a back problem."

"Oh, great catch, Emily! Is he a Baptist?"

"I just saw him once!" Emily hesitated and then added under her breath, "I think he might be a Catholic."

"What!? A Mormon would be bad enough, but a Catholic with a bad back, well, that's something altogether different!"

"Don't be so provincial. I heard him ask the desk clerk for directions to Saint Joseph's—maybe he was just meeting someone.

"Papa's gonna kill you."

"Who cares? I'll be an old maid if Papa has his way. Besides you married a Baptist and that turned out to be one big mistake."

Clara was silent. She looked down and said nothing—there was no way in the world that she was going to discuss Paul Gabriel with Emily Ann Stuart. Finally, when it appeared that Clara had nothing more to say, Emily dropped the paper she had been holding into her sister's lap, "Here, I need you to look sideways at this."

"What for?"

"He was reading it in the lobby this morning."

Although still feeling perturbed with her sister, Clara relented, "What do you want to know?"

"Tell me if he's married."

Clara held onto the newspaper, looked at it intensely until she saw multiple copies—one lining up in back of another, and another and another . . . suddenly, there was a tremendous flash of light.

HUNTSVILLE, UTAH—AMBASSADOR HOTEL LOBBY, EARLIER THAT MORNING

The transparent form of twenty-five-year-old Clara Stuart stood as eyewitness in the Ambassador Hotel lobby. The man that had captured Emily's fascination sat in one of the lobby chairs with his back to her reading the newspaper. He had a distinctive looking hat on the chair next to him and a cane leaning against the arm of his chair. Across the lobby, Clara could see her sister Emily staring into a mirror pretending to adjust her hat, but it is obvious to Clara that she was simply trying to see the man. "It looks like you had quite a time with your hat this morning," Clara stated, knowing full well Emily could hear her every word.

When the man finished reading, he stood, took his cane, walked toward the wastebasket to dispose of his paper and exited through the front door. Clara never saw the man's face, but what she did see was Emily walk over to the wastebasket and purposefully drop a handkerchief nearby. Making certain no one was watching, Emily carefully bent down to pick up both the handkerchief and the paper.

The sound of an echoing voice seemed to come to Clara's attention from far away: "What are you seeing?" Emily asked impatiently.

"Only my sister making a damn fool of herself . . . Just a minute."

Clara looked in the direction the man had gone until there was a flash of light.

HUNTSVILLE, UTAH—VESTIBULE, ST. JOSEPH'S CATHOLIC CHURCH, SAME DAY

A transparent Clara Stuart stood at the back of the

church, staring toward the altar. People entered the building and walked next to her, around her, or even through her but no one was able to see her. From the crowd it appeared that Mass was ready to start. Suddenly, Clara saw the back of the man she had been following; he was sitting in one of the Church pews near the back. The hat and cane were placed on the pew at his side.

"He's Catholic all right."

From far off in the distance, Clara could hear Emily's reply: "But is he married?"

Clara focused and imagined what the man's left hand looked like. When she could see it clearly in her mind, it was obvious that there was no ring on his finger. "He's single."

"But does he have a girlfriend?"

Just as Clara heard her sister's voice, the man turned to say something to the couple moving into the pew next to him. Clara caught her breath because it was clear that the man in church was the same man she had seen earlier that day—buck naked in nineteenth century Wyoming.

"Does he have a girlfriend?" The voice repeated.

Clara focused and looked sideways at the man until there was a tremendous burst of light.

FORT LARAMIE, WYOMING—BORDELLO ROOM, 1852

Once again, the transparent form of Clara found herself witnessing two individuals in the throes of making love upon a velvet couch. She stood off to one side of the room, simply observing. At first Clara thought she was rewitnessing the same scene from earlier in the day but there was no crib in the room and there was a big crack in the dresser mirror. In addition, a pair of nineteenth century glasses appeared to have been tossed carelessly atop the dresser. Clara looked and saw that the man was the same, but as he moved to reveal the face of the woman he was with, Clara could see that he was making love to someone who was the spitting image of Emily.

"Oh, my God!" Clara gasped, and at that moment she was brought back to Emily's apartment with the knowledge that the two of them had once slept with the same man, and that Emily had once been a dancehall girl by the name of Hannah.

HUNTSVILLE, UTAH— EMILY'S APARTMENT, 1946

Twenty-five-year-old Clara was noticeably shaken. She looked at her sister and then back at the newspaper she was holding, and finally back to her sister again.

"What's wrong with you?" Emily was obviously irritated. "Just tell me if he has a girlfriend?"

Clara was silent for the longest time. It was only when Emily looked like she was about to lose control that Clara finally managed to say, "I think he has two."

Emily angrily grabbed the newspaper out of her sister's hands. "Well, he's about to get a third!"

HUNTSVILLE, UTAH—
SUMMER MORNING, 2006

Clara Cabot leaned forward in her rocking chair, smiling. "My first day in Huntsville turned out to be quite an event. Here I had been so caught up in this divorce thing that I hadn't even thought about having another relationship. All at once I found myself certain that Emily and I were gonna be chasing after the same man . . . and a Catholic with a bad back to boot! It was a good while before I realized God doesn't give no never-mind about a person's religion."

Joan was obviously skeptical. "So Aunt Emily thought she had been with Uncle Joe before?"

"Emily didn't have any idea why she was so attracted to this soul. It was just there. And I could never bring myself to describe what I had seen. I didn't want to share Joe with someone else after he decided to start courtin' me."

The tape recorder clicked, and Joan reached over and turned the tape. When the machine was back on, she made it clear that her aunt could continue to tell the story the way she wanted to tell it.

"Okay, Clara. So, tell me about the first time you remember looking sideways."

"Oh, I think it was something I could always do." Clara Cabot reflected aloud, "It has been a part of my soul's journey for as long as I can remember. And that's a very long time, Joanie, a very, very long time indeed . . . "

THREE

SAMARIA CITY, IDAHO—
STUART FAMILY HOME, SPRING, 1932

Everett Stuart had built his two-story log farmhouse in 1920. At the same time, he had constructed a barn, a woodshed, an outhouse, and a chicken coop. Since then he had added some more fencing for the cows, goats and sheep, as well as a penned duck enclosure. Sweet potatoes, wheat and corn were his main crops, but Mabel insisted on a steady supply of tomatoes for canning, and no farm was complete without peach, cherry, apple and apricot trees. The oak tree he had planted after the house had been completed had grown a great deal in the last ten years–big enough to support a swing for the children, and Mabel had done her best to dress up the house with lace curtains, an annual flower box outside the kitchen window, and several Dorothy Parker rosebushes leading up to the front door.

Out in the wheat field, Everett Stuart appeared a good ten years older than his mid-fifties—rugged and worn from his years in the sun. He walked behind the plow and enormous horse, listening to his father, Grandfather Stuart, who walked beside him. The elderly man smoked his ever-present pipe and spoke as the two followed behind the horse.

"Son, I think you need to start thinking about Clara's education. She's got a lot of talent, that girl, and I'm certain Samaria City ain't gonna have the resources that child needs. We got to figure out how to help her now so that things are set before she graduates."

Everett shook his head, the sweat dripping from his brow; "Dad, she's only eleven. We don't have to worry about it right now. Why aren't you worried about Benjamin or Jason, or Christ, even Emily—Emily's three years older than Clara!"

"It ain't the same, son," the elder man spoke between draws on his pipe, "the boys will find their own way, and Emily is strong enough to do whatever she sets her mind on. It's Clara we gotta be thinking about."

Everett shook his head again; "Dad, the truth is Clara has always been your favorite . . . always!"

Everett turned to look his father in the eye. "Clara will do just fine. After she graduates, she'll find herself a good husband and have her own family. You'll see."

"It might turn out a little differently than you're planning." Grandfather Stuart stared out over the field and sighed.

"What's the hurry, anyway? We can talk about this a few years from now when Clara's older."

"I ain't gonna be around for that, son. I was just hoping to get things settled before I'm gone."

"Oh, Dad, you'll be here." Everett turned back to the plow and his mind returned to what he had been doing.

Grandfather Stuart had no reply.

SAMARIA CITY, IDAHO—KITCHEN, STUART FAMILY HOME, SAME DAY

Eleven-year-old Clara stood in the kitchen, staring apprehensively at the enormous pile of dishes stacked on the counter next to the washtubs—one for washing and one for rinsing. Whether it was breakfast, noontime, or supper there always seemed to be far too many dishes involved.

"I hate dishes," Clara whispered to herself, but not loud enough for her mother to hear. Mabel Stuart stood at the counter next to the pantry and kneaded four equally-sized loaves of bread dough. Four-year-old Sara was playing with a rag doll on the floor next to Clara, using an upturned Quaker Oats box as a dollhouse. Clara looked down at her sister and smiled.

"Sara, when I'm done with the dishes, you and me can go feed the ducks and then we'll have a tea party . . . "

"Don't forget you still need to weed the sweet potatoes today." Mabel Stuart reminded her.

Clara grimaced, "Yes'm, Mama."

"I want to feed a duck," Sara smiled happily.

"I promise, we'll do it later."

"Not 'til your chores are done."

"Yes'm, Mama."

The screen door slammed shut as fourteen-year-old Emily walked into the kitchen carrying an empty clothes basket. Seeing that her mother was focused on making bread, she scowled at her sister, Clara, and then stuck out her tongue.

"Mama, I think Clara forgot about weedin' the sweet potatoes," she said ever-so-sweetly.

"She knows, Emily, she knows . . . don't forget, I've got some sewing on the machine for you, and you need to sweep out the bedrooms and beat the rugs today."

"Yes, Mama."

Emily turned to her sister and mouthed the words, "I hate you," before leaving the room.

"Mama, she's doing it again," Clara protested.

"Emily Ann Stuart," came the familiar refrain but it was too late, Emily was gone.

Mabel expertly dropped each of the four kneaded loaves in a greased and floured pan. When she had eyed them all, making certain they were nearly identical in size she wiped her hands on her apron and covered the loaves with a moist dishtowel for the final rise. After looking at her youngest to make certain Sara was still preoccupied with the doll, she began to help Clara with the dishes.

"Thank you, Mama."

Mabel smiled. "So how's school, Clara?"

Clara blushed, "Paul spoke to me . . . he asked if he could borrow a pencil."

The woman appeared concerned, "The Gabriel boy? I've told you, I don't want you speaking to that boy, Clara."

"Oh, Mama!"

"I don't want you speaking to him. The family's nothing but trouble."

"Mama, it was only a pencil."

"You heard me, Clara."

"Yes'm, Mama."

When the two were silent, Sara looked up from her place on the floor and reminded Clara:

"I want to feed a duck."

"Pretty soon," was all Clara managed to say.

About three hours later the dishes had been put away and the sweet potatoes had undergone a cursory weeding—the whole process being done while Sara had played with a tiny shovel, repeatedly building a small pile of dirt and then moving it to another location about two feet away. Clara and Sara walked toward the duck enclosure; Clara held her sister's tiny hand with one set of fingers and some stale bread that their mother had given them with the other.

Grandfather Stuart stood under the oak tree smoking a pipe. Everett and his two sons—seventeen-year-old Benjamin and sixteen-year-old Jason were repairing some fencing on the far side of the horse pasture. Clara could hear the sound of Emily beating one of the house rugs beside the barn door but she refused to look in that direction. The two girls passed by the outhouse—with its shovel and its box of lime—on their way to the enclosure.

"Do you have to go to the outhouse?"

"No," Sara said positively.

"We could look at the Sears catalog," Clara added, just to make sure.

"No outhouse," Sara said positively.

"You just want to feed the ducks?"

Sara nodded joyfully.

They passed the chicken coop and ignored the chickens, which ignored them in return. As they approached the duck enclosure, surrounded on four sides and the roof with chicken wire, the ducks pressed their way to the front of the cage, knowing the presence of the girls meant bread.

"See how happy they are to see you, Sara?"

The four-year-old grinned.

Clara broke off a tiny piece of bread and handed it to her sister. Sara grabbed the bread with her tiny fingers and put it up to the chicken wire, while duck beaks attempted to push through the wire. Sara giggled and dropped the bread through the tiny wire opening, where it was quickly gobbled up. She turned to Clara, who handed her another piece of bread. The process was repeated, each time Sara cautiously putting her fingers up close enough to push the bread through the wire enclosure, but not close enough to get nibbled herself.

Finally, Sara's little fingers went between the chicken wire too far, and she was slightly nipped by one of the ducks. She immediately dropped the bread, pulled back and fell backwards onto the ground. Clara reached down to pick her up, and as she grabbed the child's hands there was a tremendous flash of light.

SAMARIA CITY, IDAHO—
STUART FAMILY HOME, FALL, 1932

The transparent form of eleven-year-old Clara stood in the doorway of her parent's room. She could see her father looking in the mirror over the dresser. He appeared unshaven and unwashed, and he kept shaking his head as he stared at his own grim reflection. His eyes were moist and the dark rings under them suggested that he had gone a very long while without sleep. Mabel Stuart lay face down on the bed, sobbing. Standing in the doorway, transparent Clara looked back and forth between her mother and father and was suddenly filled with fear and apprehension. As she wondered what could have caused such sorrow, there was a tremendous flash of light.

SAMARIA CITY, IDAHO—BAPTIST CHURCH, FALL, 1932

The Stuart family sat in the front pew, as numerous citizens from Samara City filed into the back of the church. The invisible form of eleven-year-old Clara stood against the windows, watching in wonderment as Baptists and Mormons alike came in to take a seat. Mr. and Mrs. Hurley from Hurley's Grocery and Drugstore were there. Mel Johns, owner of the Sinclair service station came in behind Mr. Harker, the Mormon Bishop. In fact, everyone that Clara knew seemed to be in attendance. She heard a couple of the women whisper such things as, "It is such a shame," or "Oh, my God, what a tragedy." But when she heard Katie Abbott's mother whisper to her eleven-year-old daughter, "Poor Mabel Stuart," Clara swung around and looked at her family sitting in the front row.

She could see her mother and father, Grandfather Stuart, Benjamin, Jason, and Emily and herself all sitting there as if they had been crying. In addition to the tears, the two things that amazed invisible Clara most of all were the fact that her two brothers were not fidgeting in their seats, and that she and Emily were sitting next to each other. Suddenly she realized that Sara was nowhere to be found, and it was then that Clara saw the tiny casket sitting up near the front of the church. Standing there invisible, she began to cry.

HUNTSVILLE, UTAH—
SUMMER MORNING, 2006

"You know, I had been the one responsible for that child. I was just the right age to help take care of her. I got to dress her for Sunday service, struggling with those hook buttonholes that Mama used to sew on our clothing. Even before that incident with the kitten, I had long wanted a child of my own . . . and Sara had finally come along. We were very close.

"Looking sideways that day, I suddenly knew something I didn't want to know—little Sara was going to die."

Clara Cabot wiped a tear from her eye, and Joan reached inside of her purse to get a Kleenex for her aunt. Even through her tears, Clara couldn't help but notice several crumpled packages of cigarettes.

"Don't worry," Joan reassured her, "I haven't been smoking on account of the baby. Are you going to be okay?"

Clara nodded, "You know, we had a little hand-me-down tea set, and Sara and I would often have a tea party, just sitting, and laughing, and being there together in the house. This is the child that came into my life. And it felt very much like she was mine. When she died, well, it just devastated all of us.

"That summer Sara was four, she started complaining about her stomach hurting. It hurt her so bad, she was crying. Mama tried ginger ale, and castor oil and mustard packs, and whatnot. Who was to know that her crying had something to do with an appendix—I had never even heard of such a thing. Sara cried and cried, and Mama was at her wit's end. Finally, Papa fetched the doctor from Malad. It was the doctor who discovered that Sara's appendix had ruptured. It was removed but it was too late."

"I'm so sorry." Joan offered another Kleenex but Clara waved it aside. "It must have been hard never seeing Sara again."

Clara seemed surprised, "Oh, I saw her a few times after she died."

"What!?"

Clara smiled. "I saw her a few times."

SAMARIA CITY, IDAHO— STUART FAMILY HOME, FALL, 1932

Eleven-year-old Clara was sitting by herself next to the duck enclosure. She wiped tears from her eyes, and sat staring at the ducks. Off in the distance, her father looked toward her and seemed to contemplate coming to get her, but he shook his head and changed his mind. As Clara cried, she started writing Sara's name in the dirt with a stick. As she retraced the letter S, more tears came to her eyes; suddenly, she heard a soft call that sounded like her name.

Clara looked up and was startled to see the transparent form of four-year-old Sara standing next to the duck enclosure, smiling back at her. Sara waved:

"Hi, Clara," came the soft sound of her four-year-old sister.

HUNTSVILLE, UTAH— SUMMER MORNING, 2006

Clara was speaking: "So often Mama had told me that these things were just my imagination, but I knew differently that day. Sara was real." Quickly, Clara changed the subject. "But it's Huntsville the Tribune wants to hear about and not some four-year-old child dying of her appendix."

Clara adjusted herself in her rocking chair, took one sip of lemonade and began again. Joan habitually glanced at her watch to see the time.

"We were on the verge of becoming another Ogden. Everyone talked about the jobs the military would be bringing in, not to mention the customers for the barbershop, and the restaurants, and the hotel. By this time, we even had a beauty salon, and I remember thinking how citified some of those women were, what with their colored nails, and all of them reading *Look* magazine beneath the dryers. Even the Emporium Theatre over on Main Street was getting the same movies they were showing over in Ogden. It was quite an exciting time for us . . . quite an exciting time.

"You know, Joanie," Clara added as an afterthought, "if I ever get depressed or unhappy about something going wrong in Clara Cabot's life, I often go there. Much of that time was simply wonderful."

FOUR

HUNTSVILLE, UTAH—HUNTSVILLE AIR FORCE BASE, MAIN ENTRANCE, 1955

Two Air Force privates finished hanging the sign on the newly erected entrance to "Huntsville Air Force Base." As they stood for a moment to admire their work, a white 1955 Ford Fairlane passed through the guard station and was saluted, as it carried the base's Colonel. The car turned onto the road leading in front of Joe and Clara Cabot's Victorian house, just beyond the base's perimeter. The Cabot home was the last one on a street, which contained a dozen houses—the final remnant of the 1920s neighborhood that had disappeared to make room for the airfield after the war. It was only in the last three years that closed door sessions somewhere in Washington, DC had given the small airfield its "Air Force Base" designation. The term had not been greeted with fanfare by anyone on Clara's street. "Who needs an Air Force base in the middle of Utah?" one of the Cabot neighbors had asked angrily. "What are we planning to do, attack Wyoming?"

The Colonel's car drove past five miles of wheat fields and scrub oak before coming to the railroad crossing that intersected Huntsville's Main Street. After the crossing, the Ford turned right onto Main and passed the beauty salon, the Emporium and Woolworth's. Just as it passed Woolworth's, a large Buick carrying a now married thirty-seven-year-old Emily and her three-year-old son parked in front of the store.

Although she was smartly dressed, Emily got out of the car with a cigarette dangling from between her lips. She reached across the front seat and took her son, helping him to his feet. "We're going to get you some new shoes today, Harold." She adjusted her glasses and made certain that any cigarette ash was brushed from her chest before walking toward the store. Finally, she took Harold by the hand and headed toward the Woolworth's entrance. Just before reaching the door, however, she saw Clara coming from the other direction.

"Emily!" thirty-four-year-old Clara Cabot said with surprise after getting over her momentary shock.

Stopping in mid-step, Emily appeared horrified and said nothing.

Clara tried again, "Emily, I know I'm not your favorite person, but don't you think we should try to make amends?

"I have nothing to say to you, Mrs. Cabot." Emily coughed with a smoker's hack. Clara reached out to touch her shoulder but Emily brushed the hand aside.

"Emily, it's been five years! It doesn't make any sense. You have a darling little boy and a husband with more money than Joe Cabot ever dreamed of. You can't still be mad at me?"

Emily simply walked around her sister and headed toward the store's entrance, dragging her son by the hand.

HUNTSVILLE, UTAH—CLARA'S VICTORIAN PORCH, LATER THAT DAY

Clara stood at the railing of her porch, watching all of the activity occurring at the base. With the sound of a massive plane flying overhead, Clara shook her head in disgust. Just then a late 1940s Ford Coupe pulled in the driveway. After a moment, thirty-eight-year-old Joe Cabot got out of the car dressed in his business attire. He walked up the porch, only lightly using his cane, approached his wife, grasped her head between his hands and kissed her first on the forehead and then on the lips.

"Hello, darlin'."

"I saw Emily today."

Joe seemed surprised, "Here at the house?"

"No, going into Woolworth's."

"Did she speak to you?"

Clara simply shook her head, "No."

Joe could see his wife was depressed, so he tried to make a joke. "Did you tell her I wasn't all you had bargained for and there'd been many a day when you would have been happy just to take me to her and drop me off on her mountain view porch?"

"She had her little boy with her," Clara sighed. "Lord, Joe, I wish we could have children."

"Me too, Clara. Me too." Joe Cabot wrapped his arm around her waist and pulled her in the direction of the front door. "Come on, darlin'. I want to tell you about work. I think I met someone we're supposed to help."

HUNTSVILLE, UTAH—SUMMER, LATE MORNING, 2006

Clara turned to her niece and emphasized what she was about to say: "You know, Joe was quite good at his job there at the railroad. He was in charge of purchasing and just loved that station. It nearly killed him when they decided to board it up. I remember it was in 1984, a couple of years after he retired. He insisted I drive him down to see it one last time. He was feeling poorly and I didn't think it was such a good idea but he got his way. That station had been such a part of his life—it likely tore out his heart when they decided to stop running the Huntsville train. I remember both of us sitting there in the car like a couple of old fools, crying. Even a Dee's hamburger didn't taste good that day."

"When did you first know you were in love with Uncle Joe?"

"Well, I guess it depends on what you mean by 'first.' I remember the day after Emily had me look sideways at that newspaper; she dragged me down to the lobby to see Joe reading his paper in person. I had been dreading this encounter ever since looking sideways for her. But I suddenly found myself in the hotel lobby, with an older sister giggling while Joe Cabot minded his business with a newspaper. There he was just reading—totally unaware that the two Stuart girls were gawking at him. He finally looked up and smiled at us . . . and when I saw his eyes, I just knew it. But even then I sensed my attraction had a lot to do with this whole business back in Fort Laramie, Wyoming."

Clara closed her eyes for a minute, as if to recall something she had seen a very long time ago. Her niece offered her some more lemonade but Clara brushed the offer aside and began her narration:

"It wasn't always called Fort Laramie. For a time it had two-to-three other names before the government decided to name it after the river. It had been built along the Oregon trail. I guess as a means of protecting the settlers going West from the Indians whose lands had been taken away from them to begin with. It was quite a wild place. In fact, locals called it 'Fort Bedlam' due to some of the goings-ons there. It had a camp for the soldiers, a general store, a mining exchange, a chapel, a legitimate hotel, and several saloons with rooms, which could be had by the night . . . or by the hour. Even had a school started one year by a chaplain name of Reverend Vaux. Serious sort of fellow, really, strict with the rules, always preaching fire and brimstone, and whatnot."

Clara appeared serious. "You know, Joanie, you're not going to want to hear this, but quite a number of folks from Clara Cabot's present found themselves back there in Fort Laramie with me . . . "

Joan grimaced, "You think they reincarnated?"

"No," Clara was firm, "I don't think it. I know it. I experienced it firsthand. I've already mentioned Joe. My father was also there, my mother, my brothers—Jason and Benjamin, my first husband—Paul, a number of others . . . and of course, Emily!" Clara sighed before beginning the tale, "You can't imagine how many eons Emily and I have been entangled with one another."

Joan put down her writing tablet and tried to appear as though she was listening.

The Reincarnation of Clara 49

FORT LARAMIE, WYOMING—FORT ENCLOSURE, 1852

Fort Laramie, Wyoming, was a place of commotion surrounded by hundreds of miles of virtually nothing, except for plains, buffalo, and the Native Sioux Indians. In addition to a storefront, a livery stable, and a blacksmith's, there was a mining exchange, a bank, a hotel, a chapel and adjoining schoolhouse, and a very large saloon. The sign out front of the saloon boasted: "Ladies entertainment, six bits." In spite of its isolated location, the fort boasted visitors from many walks of life in addition to its military troops. There were shopkeepers, farmers, cowboys, trappers, occasional families making the cross-country trek, and a few visiting Indians, not to mention the female "entertainers" at the saloon.

On the doorsteps leading to the saloon, a variety of barmaids spoke with trappers and military personnel. Among the barmaids were Clara's nineteenth century counterpart (twenty-five-year-old Esther) and Emily's nineteenth century counterpart with an ever-present rolled cigarette dangling from her lips (twenty-eight-year-old Hannah, wearing glasses). The two women looked at one another in disgust. After a moment, Esther/Clara walked back inside the saloon and was followed a short time later by Hannah/Emily.

In addition to the individuals on the porch, an occasional eager customer entered through the swinging front doors, including off-duty soldiers, trappers, and a couple of teenage boys, fearful that someone from home might see them pass inside.

In the middle of the street, out front of the saloon, a chaplain, Reverend Vaux (Clara's present-day father, Everett Stuart) was walking in the direction of a handsome, young military lieutenant, Lieutenant Martin (Clara's present-day brother, Jason), who was headed straight for the saloon.

The lieutenant was stopped by the chaplain, who placed his hand on the young man's shoulder. "Son, you're buying yourself a one-way ticket to hell faster than the devil himself."

Lieutenant Martin/Jason simply smiled, "Reverend, why don't you let yourself come in for a turn around the post with Agnes. Tell you what, it'll be my treat today."

Reverend Vaux was horrified. "Get thee behind me! The likes of you are pushing these territories lower than them heathen Injuns."

"Nothing wrong with a little Injun now and then. I've had two or three myself if you know what I mean." He gave the Reverend a knowing wink.

"You don't know what you're playing with, son!" Reverend Vaux/Everett Stuart was absolutely shocked. "We're talking about your eternal soul! Every day you come here, you're making your chances of everlasting life all the harder to come by."

"Reverend, I reckon I come into more heaven here

than you'll ever get your hands on."

The Lieutenant turned from the Reverend, removed his military gloves and looked up at a young woman smiling at him from the porch, "Afternoon, ma'am."

The Reverend was not through, "What does Commander Evans think about his men throwing their U.S. government pay down at nothing but liquor and whores?"

Lieutenant Martin smiled. "You'll have to ask him yourself, Reverend. You could probably catch him upstairs discussin' the matter with one of the girls right now."

The Reverend turned away in disgust, "If you were my son, I'd knock some sense into you, I would!" He walked back to the chapel and schoolhouse where nearly a dozen children were playing.

The Lieutenant turned into the saloon, taking the young woman on the porch by the arm.

FORT LARAMIE, WYOMING—SALOON, 1851

As was often the case, the saloon was filled with a great deal of activity (and smoke from cigarettes and cigars). An enormous mirrored bar was against the farthest wall of the saloon. One of the girls was sitting atop the bar while a customer stroked her knee with a folded piece of U.S. currency. Elsewhere, miners, trappers and disheveled soldiers sat around playing poker.

In the next century, one of the trappers would become Clara Cabot's brother, Benjamin, but at the time he had been known as Tommy. The handsomest trapper—standing more noble and appearing more groomed than the others was named Pete—nearly one hundred years later, he would become Clara's husband, Paul Gabriel, whom she divorced.

In one corner of the saloon, a roulette table and craps were positioned for those willing to place a bet. However, the major sport seemed to be poker, drinking and, of course, the women, who could be had for a price.

Hannah/Emily walked by with a cigarette dangling between her lips. She carried a couple of drinks to a poker table filled with miners. As she passed, her fanny was playfully slapped. In addition to all the noise and conversations, Mary, the oldest barmaid at the saloon sat playing piano and belting out songs for the enjoyment of a half-dozen drunken soldiers. (In the next century, Mary would become Clara's twentieth century mother, Mabel Stuart.)

Lieutenant Martin/Jason escorted his lady toward the steps and then began to ascend. At the bottom of the staircase the transparent form of an elderly Clara Cabot observed the scene. As the lieutenant went up the stairs, Esther/Clara came down with a trapper who had apparently finished his appointment. In order to pass by, Lieutenant Martin got behind his lady and Esther walked behind her gentleman, single file. The lieutenant tipped his hat to Esther as he passed and said with a smile, "Afternoon, Ma'am."

Esther was flirtatious. "Afternoon, Lieutenant."

When Esther got to the bottom of the stairs she passed by the transparent version of Clara. Her customer went on ahead towards the bar. For a moment, Esther turned, as if expecting to see somebody. She stared in the direction of Clara but was unable to see anything—in spite of feeling as though something or someone unseen was there.

As she turned, she ran into the handsome trapper, Pete/Paul Gabriel, and the two stared at one another. Very quickly, however, the trapper's own barmaid companion angrily pulled him by the arm. "Come on, Pete," she demanded, causing him to reluctantly follow her up the stairs.

When Esther turned toward the bar, she nearly ran into Hannah who was coming back with a full tray of drinks.

"Trail Bitch!" Hannah called her.

Esther ignored her. As she passed, she was firmly patted on the backside by Tommy/Benjamin: "Hey, Esther, how 'bout fetchin' me and the boys here another whiskey?"

"Anything for you boys," Esther said, remaining in character.

FORT LARAMIE, WYOMING—BORDELLO ROOM, LATER THAT YEAR

Esther/Clara was sitting propped up in bed, leaning back against the pillows with her covers drawn haphazardly around her chest. Russell/Joe Cabot stood off to one side, lifting his pants off the red velvet couch in order to get dressed.

"When will I see you again?" Esther asked, sounding somewhat downhearted.

"I thought you always knew when I was coming around?"

She shrugged, "Can you come tonight?"

Russell shook his head, "Can't make any promises, darlin'." He turned to check out his appearance in the mirror, before taking some bills out of his wallet and placing the money on top of the nightstand.

"Oh, Russ, you don't have to do that!"

"I pay my own way, darlin'." He winked to show her that she was still special.

Esther relented, "When do you think you'll be back at Laramie?"

"Can't say for certain. American Fur Company asked me to set up a trading party with the Cheyenne before month's end—we'll see how it goes."

Although she appeared cautious, Esther finally said, "Can I ask you something, Russell?

"Darlin', you can ask me anything."

"You been spending time with Hannah?"

"Maybe once or twice, Esther, but you see other men." The remark caused her to frown, so he added: "I tell ya what, darlin', it don't mean nothin', you're the only girl for me."

Russell leaned down and grasped her head between his hands, kissing her on the forehead and then upon the lips. After he departed, Esther was left alone in her room.

She reached over to the nightstand and grabbed her robe, putting it on as she got out of bed. She walked over to the dresser, gently touching the money he had left. Afterwards, she picked up the brush to comb her hair, staring at her own reflection in the mirror. Suddenly, her reflection dissolved into the image of herself holding a baby girl.

The image caused Esther to catch her breath, and the reflection dissolved until she saw only herself staring back from the mirror.

"Damn," she said, dropping the brush on top of the dresser. "I'm pregnant."

HUNTSVILLE, UTAH—SUMMER, LATE MORNING, 2006

Clara stopped rocking the chair, and leaned in the direction of her niece. "What I wouldn't have given to have a child in this life." She looked at Joan and then added, "Just imagine how closely we're all connected from one lifetime to the next. You know, that child in

Fort Laramie would return as my younger sister, Sara."

"Sara had been your child in Laramie?"

Clara nodded, "I essentially abandoned her in Laramie, without giving it a second thought. This time around, she had to abandon me . . . the Bible calls it, 'What you sow you reap.'"

Joan sat quietly, watching her aunt in disbelief before adding, "Don't you think this sounds a little crazy?"

"Only if you don't know any better." Clara continued, "You know, the one thing I really ever wanted in this life was the one thing I just couldn't have. I remember growing up and wanting, more than anything, to be a mother. Emily and my brothers were interested in school and educating themselves and moving beyond the business of farming but I had a whole different life in mind. I was going to be a wife and a mother, raise five children and grow old with my very own family. Now all I've done is grown very old.

"I have to tell you, Joanie, in spite of what Emily, or Benjamin, or Jason thought about it, I never did like school. The other girls seemed to take pleasure in teasing me unmercifully. Maybe they were afraid of me. Maybe they thought I was too different. Whatever the reason, I remember this whole business of school was a very challenging time in my life. "

SAMARIA CITY, IDAHO—CLARA'S SCHOOLYARD, LATE SPRING, 1932

Clara was eleven. A number of boys played baseball during recess in a large field (with bleachers off to one side), while a number of girls played jump rope or simply appeared more interested in standing around to talk. Clara sat by herself on the first row of bleachers. She pretended not to notice that a couple of the other girls, including Katie Abbott, were laughing and pointing at her. Instead, Clara directed her eyes back and forth between the ground and fourteen-year-old Paul Gabriel, who played ball.

In all, approximately thirty children between the ages of ten and thirteen were at recess. A group of boys played marbles on the blacktop near the schoolhouse or tried to exchange their marbles (and 'biggies' and 'shooters') with others. Nearby, some of the girls played hopscotch or jacks. Scattered throughout the playground, several teachers monitored the activities. Mr. Burnett, the gym teacher, was among them, wearing a shiny whistle on a cord dangling from his neck.

As she sat, Clara toyed with a stick and couldn't stop herself from looking at Paul, whose team was at bat. Slowly, she drew the name "Paul" in the dirt, and then encircled it with a heart. Katie and the other girls continued to point at her and giggle.

Oblivious to the presence of the others, Clara continued to draw in the dirt. She drew an "1," and then a

"3," and finally she wrote the word "home." Somehow Clara knew the outcome of each boy's success at the plate before he even swung the bat. However, the act was unconscious, for Clara remained spellbound by Paul's every move, and waited for his turn at bat.

Katie Abbott nodded to her friends before walking quietly atop the third row of bleachers, attempting to sneak in back of Clara in order to discover what the pitiful creature had been writing. When Katie stood just behind Clara, she was delighted to spot the name "Paul" and the heart. However, it wasn't long before Katie realized what the numbers were all about. Clara continued to write each boy's success at bat even before the ball was thrown. Clara wrote a "2" for the player just before Paul, and when the boy stopped at second, Katie Abbott suddenly opened her mouth in horror and disbelief:

"Devil child! Devil child!" Katie pointed at Clara accusingly before running back to tell the other girls what she had just witnessed.

Immediately, Clara took her stick and scribbled out everything that she had been writing. Once again, she felt very different than the other children, and knew that she was very much alone.

SAMARIA CITY, IDAHO—CLARA'S SCHOOLYARD, FALL, 1934

Thirteen-year-old Clara Stuart sat by herself on the

first row of bleachers. She had waited until all of the boys had gone inside from their football practice, as she was afraid of being ridiculed by Katie or one of the others. When it came to Paul Gabriel, she couldn't help but look at him, which had caused a fair measure of embarrassment on several occasions. Just two weeks previously, that horrible Gladys Hooper had gone up to Paul and told him loud enough for everyone to hear: "I think Clara Stuart has a big crush on you, Paul!" Paul had looked at Gladys like she was crazy but everyone else had started laughing. It had been just awful.

Clara was still horrified by the memory, and she shook her head to erase it from her mind. She thought about toying with a stick and writing in the dirt, but she might lose track of what she was writing and get into even more trouble. She was certain that Gladys had gone up to Paul because it was Gladys Hooper herself who had a crush on Paul, and she had only used Clara as an excuse to talk to him; still it had been quite embarrassing. So what if she wanted to stare at Paul? What difference did it make? Why couldn't she just stare at Paul whenever she wanted and be left alone?

And it was at that moment that the idea finally came to her. Maybe she could stare at Paul after all? Maybe she could do it when she was all alone with no one else watching!

Clara adjusted herself on the bench and closed her

eyes. She took a breath and relaxed, and then took another breath. In her imagination she pretended she could see Paul standing in the boys' locker room. She imagined she could see him standing there by one of the lockers. She imagined what he looked like just after the practice game. She focused as hard as she could to see Paul's face, and she took another breath, imagined some more and suddenly she saw a brilliant flash of light.

SAMARIA CITY, UTAH—CLARA'S SCHOOL, BOYS' LOCKER ROOM, 1934

The transparent form of thirteen-year-old Clara Stuart stood in the boys' locker room. It wasn't much more than a large bathroom with showers, but to her amazement Clara found herself standing in the middle of a bunch of boys—hearing their voices, smelling the odors of sweat and water and steam, and seeing twenty boys in every imaginable state of undress.

At first she froze in fear, worried that the boys would be able to see her, but when it became clear that they were totally ignorant of her presence (and even Clara could see through her transparent arm) she stared at them with wide-eyed fascination.

Yes, she had older brothers and, yes, she had seen them both wearing nothing but towels, but this was quite a different sensation. She had never really wanted to look at her brothers, now Clara found herself wanting to look. And look she did.

She saw Tom Stevens standing with his back to her as he took a shower. Clara couldn't help but stare as she watched the water cascade over his shoulders, flow down his back, and slide around the pale white curves of his bottom. Her eyes opened wide and she kept staring.

A moment later, Mitchell Hankins walked right next to her as naked as the day he was born on his way to the shower. It was the first human penis she had ever seen, bringing two thoughts immediately to mind: why did Mitchell scratch it like that in front of everyone, and why was the thing so much smaller than the ones she had seen on the horse, the ram, and even the dog? She couldn't help but watch his every move as Mitchell turned on the shower and stood there, letting the water flow over the place he had been scratching. It was then that Tom Stevens turned off the water and turned around and Clara could see that in spite of the fact that Tom was about six inches taller, both he and Mitchell were about the same size in the penis department. The awareness made her wonder if all boys were the same and human penises came in only one size.

Clara heard a slight commotion behind her and turned to see that five or six boys—some wearing towels and others shorts—were standing around another boy who was sitting on one of the wooden benches next to the lockers. She thought about investigating but decided that this was her opportunity to see Paul Gabriel—to really see Paul Gabriel. She turned around twice looking everywhere for him when she suddenly realized that the boy on the bench was Paul. She walked over to the group just as one of the boys in a towel spoke to Paul:

"Paul, are you going to be all right? Do you want me to get Mr. Burnett?"

It was then that Clara could hear the sounds of Paul's wheezing, as he struggled to get his breath. She managed to peer between two of the boys and get a glimpse of Paul, just as he motioned his hand back and forth to say, "No." But his wheezing continued.

"Asthma," one of the boys whispered to the one next to him.

Finally, Paul managed to say with a shortness of breath, "I'll be fine."

He started to stand and one of his friends encouraged him to wait, but Paul just pushed the boy aside. In spite of his heavy breathing, he walked in the direction of the shower, threw his towel on the floor and turned to give Clara the most amazing sight she had ever seen.

Although he was light-skinned and fair-haired, his groin was covered with the curliest black hair Clara had ever seen. It was also immediately clear that Paul was a little bigger in the penis department than either the Mitchell or Hankins boys.

"They *don't* come in one size," Clara whispered to

herself. And then she was silent. The whole while Paul showered she just stared and stared. In spite of the fact that she knew she wasn't physically there, she started to feel very, very warm.

She watched him wash his hair, put soap in his armpits and all over his chest. She caught her breath as he put soap in between the creases of his buttocks and then repeatedly lathered up his penis and groin. She got to watch nearly the whole procedure until, finally, she heard the sound of her own name being spoken way off in the distance: "Clara . . . " and suddenly she felt her real self shaken back on the bleachers so that Paul, the boys' locker room, and all of her surroundings instantly disappeared.

SAMARIA CITY, IDAHO—CLARA'S SCHOOLYARD, FALL, 1934

"Clara, what in the hell are you doing here?" sixteen-year-old Emily said angrily. "I've been looking all over for you."

Clara gave no response.

"Why didn't you answer me when I called?"

It took another moment, before Clara was able to answer, "I . . . I think I was just daydreaming."

"You've got to be pretty stupid to be sitting out here all alone!" Emily was exasperated. "How the hell did I ever get a sister like you?"

"Momma said not to cuss."

"Oh shut up," Emily replied, grabbing her sister by the hand and pulling her to her feet. "It's time to go home."

FORT LARAMIE, WYOMING—SALOON, SUMMER, 1852

It was evening at the saloon, and all the regulars had found their respective places. Mary/Mabel Stuart sang at the piano, trying hard to raise the sound of her voice over drunken revelers and card players fixated on poker. Esther/Clara was obviously about 8 months pregnant. She walked by the roulette wheel and whispered under her breath, "Seventeen," just moments before the rotating ball finally dropped and came to a stop in 17 black. Esther nodded with approval. She appeared disheveled, with her hair drooping on either side of her face. She had been waitressing for most of the evening.

In fact, for several months now Esther's physical state had relegated her to waitressing alone—longer hours and fewer tips than could be had up the stairs. Just as bad was the fact that many of the other barmaids now treated her with some measure of disdain. She finished serving a round of drinks next to the piano—receiving a good butt slap in return before wiping her brow with her palm. At the same moment, Mary finished her song and rose from the piano stool, calling out to those nearest her: "Time to take a break, fellas."

The Reincarnation of Clara 65

One of the men, named Rudy, bellowed with some measure of disappointment, "Don't be gone too long, Mary. Soon as I win me a hand, I'll be escorting you up them stairs."

Mary was quick to reply: "Fine, Rudy, but would you mind going up and starting without me? I've had you and I've had the piano and, frankly, I think the piano gives me a better time." Two of the players at Rudy's table laughed and lifted a toast to Mary in response. Afterwards, Mary walked over to Esther and put her arm around the back of the pregnant woman.

"You okay, girl?"

"Just tired," she sighed. "Tired of workin', tired of workin' here, and tired of all the girls but you. Mary, I don't know what I would do if I didn't have you to talk to."

"Never been pregnant myself, but can't imagine it's much of a county fair."

"It is hard to take your mind off of it, that's for sure." She patted the sides of her enormous belly. "I'm the size of a buffalo."

"Honey, if I were you I'd just drape the mirror in my room and not give it a second thought." Mary became serious for a moment, "Esther, I'm worried about you. What are you going to do? This is no place for a child."

"I keep hoping that Russell's gonna decide to take me out of the Wyoming territory altogether."

"What about the baby?"

Esther simply shrugged her shoulders, "I don't know. Russell doesn't think the plains are any place for a young 'un. Real trouble is he doesn't know if the baby's his."

"Is it?"

"I think so . . . I don't know! I wasn't expecting to get pregnant."

"Well, what are you going to do, girl? You gotta think of something soon."

Russell/Joe appeared at the top of the saloon stairs with Hannah/Emily as his escort. The two had obviously finished their business. He turned to give the woman one last kiss on the lips before heading down the steps. Hannah had to remove her cigarette in order to kiss him. Afterwards, she took a long drag before coming down the stairs to the bar. When she passed by Esther, she shook her head in disgust and stated for the hundredth time: "You have to be pretty stupid to get yourself pregnant without a husband!"

"Go fuck yourself," Esther replied.

"You're too far gone to even try to do it to yourself," was the response.

Before any more could be said, one of the whiskered fur traders grabbed his fiddle from under the table and began to play a jig. A couple of soldiers, scouts, and frontiersmen began slapping their legs in tune with the music. One of the trappers jumped up from his seat, pushed his chair aside, grabbed Esther by the hand and began twirling her around the table.

The dance between a very pregnant Esther and the scruffy trapper provided a great deal of entertainment for some of the other customers, who stopped what they are doing and begin to watch, clap and cheer. Commotion began to rise throughout the saloon, and the evening was still young.

HUNTVILLE, UTAH—THE BERTHANA (DANCE HALL), 1948

Twenty-seven-year-old Clara Cabot danced with a clean-shaven stranger (who had once been a whiskered-faced trapper from the Ft. Laramie saloon) in the middle of a 1940s ballroom. Joe Cabot sat at a table and watched his wife with appreciation. After a dance or two, he was generally through for the night. Joe's cane had been placed under his own chair. One thing was certain—Clara could dance. About thirty-five smartly dressed couples waltzed around the dance floor listening to the music of an eight-piece band (which included a former fiddle-playing fur trader from the nineteenth century) situated on a stage off to one side. Other individuals mingled around the outskirts of the dance floor or simply sat, listening to the music. The floor was polished hardwood, surrounded on all sides by folding chairs for those who listened, as well as for the 'wall-flowers'. As was always the case at the Berthana, everyone was dressed to the hilt.

The Berthana Dance Hall was on the second floor of an enormous three-story brick building on Huntsville's Main Street. The first floor was a music store during the day. Every day of the week, except Sunday, the second and third floors at the Berthana came to life. The second floor was for music and dancing, and on the third floor refreshments could be had. If you were looking for a dance, a night out, or even the possibility of finding a spouse, the Berthana was the place to be.

HUNTSVILLE, UTAH—SUMMER, LATE MORNING, 2006

"Oh, I just loved to dance," Clara Cabot reflected aloud. "The first time I put my foot out on that floor . . . well, I thought I'd gone to heaven. You see, being Baptists and all, Mama didn't believe in dancing. When I was in High School and there'd be a dance, all the Mormon girls would get a dance card tied around their wrists. During the program, the boys would come up and ask for a dance. Well, if you wanted to dance with that boy you'd write his name down for some point in the evening; if you didn't want to dance, you just politely said that your card was full. I used to wish Mama would let me go but it wasn't allowed. I didn't get to dance until I got to Huntsville.

"Emily had gone to the Berthana a couple of times

with some friends from work, that's how I first heard about it. Let me tell you, Joanie, your Aunt Emily could sew and she could cook but she couldn't dance her way off of the sidewalk. That girl had two left feet!" Clara tapped the table in order to get the reporter's attention. "Of course, Emily had gone to Shorty Ross's Berthana looking for a man, not for the music. She was much more interested in a bed warmer than she was in tap shoes." Clara chuckled. "But after Joe and I got together, I think Emily stopped going to the Berthana altogether. I don't think she wanted to take the chance of running into the two of us.

"Before and after we were married, Joe used to take me to the Berthana a couple nights a week . . . you paid a dollar to get in, and could dance 'til midnight if you wanted to. Joe could only dance a couple of rounds because of his leg but he used to encourage me to dance with some of the other men. You know, there was a time if I couldn't dance I wasn't fit to live with. Joe used to laugh at me and say, 'My God, Clara, you'd dance 'til sun-up if the band kept playing!'

"Shorty's band could play anything, whether it was a waltz or a beer barrel polka; your feet wanted to get out on that floor. A couple a times a year we'd get a traveling band at the Berthana like Mike Riley and his group . . . once we even got Guy Lombardo and the Royal Canadians; 'course it was a dollar-fifty more to get in.

"You dressed like ladies and gentleman back then. Men always had a suit and tie, and ladies had their dancing pumps and a dress that was floor-length or down to their ankles." She chuckled, "I tell you, back then jeans were something a fella wore to work on his car. I remember my first Green-Gold Ball. I wore a pretty taffeta that I got at Penney's, and Joe looked so handsome in his dark brown suit. You know, I bought that dress for three-and-a-half-dollars!

"When you got tired, you went upstairs for a soda pop. They didn't serve liquor—this being Mormon country and all—'course some of the fellas would bring 'a bottle on the hip' and then buy a soda as a mix. It was okay with the Berthana—that's just the way things were done. We didn't get drunk or anything—the bottle was just a half a pint, and we didn't go to the Berthana for drinking or smooching, you went there for dancing.

"They served popcorn at your table but for real eats we'd go to the Star Noodle Parlor in Ogden. The Bamburger Trolley could have you to twenty-fourth street from Shorty's in under twenty minutes. That ride into Ogden was only five cents."

Clara poured herself what was left of the lemonade and took a sip, while Joan wrote down some notes pertaining to what her aunt had just described.

"Years later when Joe and I had got too old for dancing, and the Berthana had long been torn down, we'd sit in the living room and watch Lawrence Welk and think of how much fun we used to have. We'd see 'em all slicked-up on the television just like when we were young. You know, nothing used to shape-up a TV-tray dinner finer than Lawrence Welk."

"Didn't Uncle Joe mind you dancing with other men?"

Clara looked surprised and then started chuckling. "Well, you make it sound much more interesting than it was. Every week there would be two or three men sitting around in the chairs just hoping to step out on the floor with someone. Joe would make certain that they got at least one turn around the deck. He used to tell me, 'Clara, it just seems proper that everybody gets a dance.' He was always thinking of others . . . Joe was like that. You know, over the years quite a number of times he'd bring someone home from work that needed help. Didn't matter if it was an employee, a passenger, or even a hobo. If Joe Cabot found they were in trouble, he'd bring them home and we'd work together."

"What did you do?" Joan appeared curious.

"Mostly we'd all just talk. Joe had a way of putting them right at ease . . . 'course in the middle of serving lunch or lemonade or whatnot, Joe would have me 'look sideways' at the problem and get right to the heart of it. Mind you, I didn't come right out and discuss what I was doing. By this time I'd learned to keep my mouth shut, but somehow there was always something I could work into the conversation and help set things right. Now, Joe didn't tell these people, 'I'm gonna take you home, and we're gonna have lunch, and my wife's gonna look sideways at you,' but that's what happened. They'd come to the house and in the course of the conversation things would just start to seem more reasonable. Looking sideways doesn't always solve the issue, but it can sure give you clarity in terms of what in the world is going on.

"You know, a number of times we'd have a young person in . . . turn out to be a runaway. I'd help them see clear to going home, and Joe would buy 'em a ticket for the bus and send them home with money in their pocket. Working together like that was kind of fun. One thing for certain, I think it cleared up a lot of the selfishness we couldn't see our way past in Laramie. We cleared up a lot of karma, Joe and I."

FIVE

HUNTSVILLE, UTAH—CLARA'S VICTORIAN HOME, SEPTEMBER, 1952

Clara Cabot laid out the finishing touches on her lunch table, as Joe would be bringing the young woman home from work any minute. It wasn't a fancy lunch, but it would be filling: tuna fish sandwiches, the last of the summer tomatoes, a chilled cantaloupe and Kool-Aid. Clara actually preferred sun tea but the young woman was Mormon, "And no self-respecting Mormon will drink tea," she whispered under her breath. She had almost served Jell-O, as it was a Utah staple, but the melon was perfectly ripe and needed to be eaten in the next day or two.

Clara expected them just after 2:30. A late lunch for

sure, but Joe had said that Ruth Adams worked in the café for both the breakfast and lunch shifts and couldn't leave until about a quarter past 2:00. "Not a problem," Clara had assured him. Both she and Joe looked forward to these looking–sideways activities.

"She's really nothing more than a young girl, darlin'," Joe had told her the night before. "Her mother died about 8 months ago from a horrible bout with breast cancer. Never met her father but I know his name is Murray. Rumor is he was a drinker before his wife died and that alcohol has only become more of a problem since then."

"Isn't he Mormon?" Clara was surprised.

"You can be an alcoholic and still be a Mormon, Clara." Joe assured her. "Anyway, Ruth has seemed very, very depressed. Before her mother died, we always exchanged words when I'd get my morning coffee or we'd have a little conversation when I ate my Friday lunch in the café but lately she keeps pretty much to herself. She never smiles any more and seems to be in her own little world. It's obvious she's not happy, Clara. I think she needs our help."

Clara had just finished repeating the conversation in her head when she heard Joe's car pull in the driveway—a sound that was quickly replaced by the roar of a jet engine overhead. Clara finished arranging the table one last time, and brushed her hands against her apron just as Joe opened the door and ushered the young woman in.

The Reincarnation of Clara 75

"Well, aren't you a pretty little thing?" The words came quickly out of Clara's mouth. "Joe didn't mention you were so lovely!" The young woman was average in height but nothing else about her was average. She had a perfect figure, her blonde hair with its natural highlights had been pulled back behind her ears, highlighting the perfect angles of her face, and her eyes were the most stunning green Clara had ever seen.

Ruth Adams gave a slight grin but her eyes remained downcast on the carpet. "Thank you for inviting me to lunch, ma'am." In spite of the fact she wore no makeup, kept her blouse buttoned up to her neck, had a hard time smiling, and didn't look people in the eyes, Ruth Adams could not hide her beauty.

"Oh, please call me Clara." She took the young woman by the arm and led her toward the table. "I love having people over from the railroad—it allows me to meet all the nice folks that Joe has been talking about. That way, I get to participate in his work. Otherwise, there's not much to talk about but the TV." Clara smiled. "Speaking of TV, did you watch Senator Nixon from California on the TV last night, Ruth?"

"No, ma'am, but my aunt lives in California. I'm sure she saw it."

"An aunt," Clara commented aloud. "Is that your mother's sister?"

"Yes, ma'am. She came for the funeral but I don't get to see her that often."

"Well it was quite a speech. I think he came across rather good, don't you, Joe?"

Joe shrugged, "Well darlin', I still think the man's a crook. Even if he didn't do anything illegal, there's something about him that seems sneaky. And, personally, I don't care about his dog, Checkers."

"He'll be in the White House," Clara was adamant.

Joe seemed surprised. "As Vice President? Eisenhower's going to win?"

"Well, yes, Eisenhower's going to win but I mean Nixon will be in the White House on his own. Some day Richard Nixon will be President."

"No!" Joe appeared shocked. "He can't win the presidency after all this!"

"He *will* be President," Clara assured him.

She led Ruth to a chair, which Joe pulled back for her until the young woman sat. He then pushed her chair in and he and Clara took their seats. As was his habit, Joe put his cane under his chair.

"Ruth been working in the café for just about a year now," Joe stated matter-of-factly. "She knows all the regulars."

"Oh, that's wonderful!" Clara poured them each a glass of Kool-Aid and then started passing the sandwiches, tomatoes, and cantaloupe. "How do you work at the café and go to school at the same time?"

"I dropped out, ma'am. School just wasn't for me." Ruth never lifted her eyes from the table.

"Maybe you're just taking a break," Clara smiled at

her. She watched Ruth take a sandwich and looked over at Joe.

"You're so personable, Ruth," Joe complimented. "You have the ability to make everybody comfortable around you—I've seen you do it. You're also very attractive. Any company would be lucky to have you."

Ruth made no reply, and instead kept her eyes focused on her plate.

"Do you know what you want to do with your life?" Joe inquired.

The reply was barely audible. "Not really."

"Well, there's still time." Joe sounded positive but he looked toward Clara and winked. That was their signal.

Clara finished chewing the bite of sandwich, nodded and asked the young woman, "Tell me about your mother."

Ruth didn't say anything immediately; still Clara watched her intently. In fact, Clara watched the younger woman until Ruth's features began to blur. Soon, identical images of Ruth Adams began to appear, as if they were superimposed one right behind the other.

Just as the girl began to speak, Clara saw a tremendous flash of light.

HUNTSVILLE, UTAH—RUTH ADAM'S PARENTS' HOME, JANUARY, 1952

Although it was midday, the bedroom blinds remained drawn, casting long afternoon shadows on each of the four walls. Ruth Adams sat next to her mother's bedside, wiping the woman's forehead with a cool washcloth. Bernice Adams was in the final stages of breast cancer. In spite of radical, disfiguring surgery and the morphine that the doctors had provided, Bernice was dying and she was in pain. The transparent form of Clara Cabot stood as a quiet bystander against one of the bedroom walls.

"I love you, Momma," Ruth said, trying hard to hold back the tears. "I love you so much."

Although Bernice's eyes were three-quarters closed, she began to smile, "I love you too, sweetie." The woman then shivered as a sharp pain went through her back and she let out a soft moan.

"Do you need some pills, Momma?"

Bernice shook her head and waved the statement aside with her right hand as she reached out to take her daughter's hand. Although she was sick, the stunning features that she had passed on to her daughter could almost be seen in spite of the woman's pale complexion and her dark, sunken eyes. "Where is your father?"

"He said he had to go for a drive, Momma. He said he'd come back soon."

"I need you to promise to take care of him, Ruth. He's been through a lot."

"Yes, Momma."

"When I'm gone, he'll have nobody but you to make sure he's all right."

"Yes, Momma." Ruth began to cry.

"Promise me you'll take care of him, Ruth."

"I promise."

"Can you hold me, Ruthie? I want you to hug your Momma." The dying woman smiled and opened her eyes as best as she could.

Clara Cabot silently watched the scene, and although these were images of the past, she couldn't help but wipe away a few tears.

HUNTSVILLE, UTAH—RUTH ADAM'S PARENTS' HOME, 3½ MONTHS LATER

Clara Cabot found herself standing in another darkened bedroom in the Adams' home. This time, however, it was Ruth's room and not her mother's. Clara stood right next to the bed and could see that the young woman had curled herself up, with the covers pulled all the way to her chin. Even in the dark, Clara could see that Ruth Adams had been crying.

"It's only natural, honey," Clara whispered in her head; after all, the girl's mother had only been dead a short time.

All at once the lights from a car flashed past the

window as a vehicle came to a quick stop in the driveway. The brakes squeaked just as Ruth cringed. A moment later, Clara could hear the sound of the front door being opened and someone bumping into an end table or some piece of furniture in the living room.

"Oh, shit!" came the voice from the hallway.

A few moments later, Ruth's bedroom door was opened, and the silhouette of her father stood quietly for a moment as he looked in at his daughter. Immediately, the smell of alcohol pervaded the room.

"Are you awake, Ruthie?" her father asked.

Ruth Adams remained completely still and said nothing.

"Are you awake?"

When there came no reply, her father began unbuttoning his shirt. He removed his shirt, shoes, socks, slacks and underwear and then slurred as he spoke: "I need to sleep with you tonight, honey." Without saying another word, Murray Adams crawled into bed, completely naked, with his own daughter.

Clara Cabot gasped.

HUNTSVILLE. UTAH—CLARA'S VICTORIAN HOME, SEPTEMBER, 1952

Joe Cabot finished his sandwich and looked back and forth between his wife and Ruth Adams. Clara appeared quite startled, so he knew that his wife was

The Reincarnation of Clara *81*

back. While Clara had been off looking sideways, Ruth had been talking about her mother, and Joe had responded with a question or two. Ruth had just finished telling about how much she and her mother had loved being with each other in the Ward's Relief Society, socializing and being of service with other Mormon women in their church.

"I haven't been to Relief Society since Momma got very sick," Ruth sighed. "Of course, all the women in the church have been very helpful to Poppa and me all along."

"Ruth, you need to leave your father's house." Clara's words were spoken with compassion but they were firm.

Ruth was so surprised by the statement that she finally looked at Clara Cabot, making eye contact. "I promised Momma that I would take care of him."

"Your Momma did not want this for you!"

Ruth began to cry. All the tears that had been pent-up inside the girl began to come out. Clara immediately got up from her chair and hurried around to embrace the young woman in her arms. Ruth sobbed uncontrollably. Joe looked completely confused, and didn't know what to do.

"Her father's been raping her," Clara finally said.

Joe Cabot's mouth fell open in disbelief.

HUNTSVILLE, UTAH—SUMMER, LATE MORNING, 2006

"It was just heartbreaking what Murray Adams had been doing to his daughter," Clara repeated, shaking her head in dismay.

"What did you and Uncle Joe do to help her?" Joan was obviously quite interested in this part of the story.

"Well, we had Ruth stay with us for a couple of days. We called her aunt in California, and Joe went out and spoke with Murray."

"What did he say?"

"I wasn't there, honey, but Joe told me he made it quite clear that Murray Adams was not to come to our house looking for his daughter. Joe and I decided the best place for the girl was in California, so we took $500 out of our savings account, which was quite a sum of money in those days, bought Ruth a ticket, gave her some money, and made all the arrangements with her aunt. Ruth Adams went out west, where she could start over.

"Your Uncle Joe told Murray that he wasn't to go to California after her or else we'd have to involve the authorities . . . Imagine, raping your own daughter!"

Joan grimaced as the baby moved in her belly. After readjusting herself in the chair and trying to get as comfortable as possible for a woman in her condition, she asked, "Do you know what happened to Ruth, or her father?"

"Ruth made a new life for herself. She finished high school—even went on to college, where she graduated with a degree in child psychology. She joined a practice out there somewhere near Anaheim. She got married and raised two kids of her own." Clara Cabot tapped a boney finger on the table, as if to emphasize her point. "In spite of what she'd been through, Ruth Adams made a wonderful life for herself helping others . . . I still get a Christmas card from her every year."

"What about Murray Adams?"

"Well, your Uncle Joe really tried to help him with this alcohol problem, but he was on and off the wagon for years. I don't think he ever got over his wife's death, and then the guilt over what he had done to his daughter must have been awful. Ruth came out here once to confront him about it—part of her own therapy, I believe. After that, there was some reconciliation and they were cordial. Ruth told me they spoke on the phone about once every other month or so, and I know he went to California once and even went to Disneyland with his grandkids, but he was never quite right. I think he took his guilt and the depression all the way to the grave. Murray Adams has been dead for at least twenty years now. It was such a waste."

Clara became quiet for a moment of contemplation before adding: "Joanie, if only we could see how each of our choices sets in motion a chain of events that we will have to face. You know, the greatest thing that any soul can do is to just put someone else's needs before their own. Just being kind—that's what it's all about. That's why we're here . . . too bad most of us need a good knock up side the head before the message gets through."

Clara reached for her glass and could see that both it and the pitcher were empty. She glanced over at her niece, as the younger woman finished jotting down some notes. When Joan finally looked up from what she had been writing, Clara smiled and motioned towards the front door.

"Why don't we go inside and have some lunch, Joanie? I've made some tuna fish."

"That sounds nice, Aunt Clara." Finally, Joan E. Stuart managed a smile in return.

FORT LARAMIE, WYOMING—BORDELLO ROOM, SEPTEMBER, 1852

The transparent form of eighty-five-year-old Clara Cabot stood like a quiet sentinel, silently watching the same scene she had visited quite a number of times before. She knew that this particular experience had been instrumental in her life as Esther, becoming the impetus that prompted her to abandon her child in Fort Laramie and ultimately created the karmic memory that led to her loss of little Sara. She turned to see the child's crib set off in one corner of the room—the baby girl was fast asleep. The worst thing about being witness to the past was the inability to change it. The second disadvantage was being unable to interact with the things that she saw—how Clara longed to pick up that child who would become Sara and cuddle the baby in her arms. But all she could do was watch.

The couple on the couch continued their lovemaking and were close to reaching climax. Esther/Clara let out several short, stifled moans, letting her head fall back over the arm of the couch, while she arched her back. When she finally sighed, Russell/Joe knew his time had come. His own movements became more intense until he finally let loose the noise that always sounded like he was trying to muffle himself so that no one else might hear. After his climax, he fell on top of Esther, grasped her head between his hands, kissed her on the forehead and then the lips. As he rose from the couch, he smiled.

"Been a while, darlin', but you haven't forgotten a thing."

Esther smiled back at him, said nothing and pulled on her robe as he began to dress. She watched him put on his clothes and shook her head in frustration when he laid money on top of the dresser. She decided the time had come to speak what had long been on her mind.

"Russ, I'm giving up the business . . . I'm not seeing anyone but you."

Russell appeared somewhat startled, "What are you saying, Esther?"

"Are you ever going to take me with you?"

"I've told you before, territory's no place for a kid."

"I love you, Russ." She said it aloud, for the very first time.

At first he seemed as though he might say something else but instead he repeated, "Territory's no place for a kid." Without saying another word, Russell turned and left the room. Esther looked to the door, glanced toward the crib, and then back at the door again.

"I'm coming with you, Russ, so you better get used to the idea!" Esther said loudly, and then added: "There's got to be a way."

Suddenly her baby began to cry.

SAMARIA CITY, IDAHO—STUART FAMILY HOME, HALLWAY OUTSIDE SARA'S BEDROOM, FALL, 1932

Eleven-year-old Clara sat on the floor outside her little sister's bedroom. She held her knees to her chest, gently rocking and trying to comfort herself. The soft, whimpering sounds of four-year-old Sara were heard coming from the room. Clara's mother and Father were whispering with the doctor, who was in attendance.

Finally, Mabel Stuart came out into the hallway, appearing depressed and sullen.

"Clara, why don't you go outside and see what your brothers are doing?"

Clara did not move; instead she looked back toward little Sara's room.

"Go on, Clara. You can't do anything right now."

After hesitating for a moment, Clara nodded and rose to her feet. She walked down the hallway and reached the top of the stairs.

SAMARIA CITY, IDAHO—STUART FAMILY HOME, TOP OF STAIRS, ONE YEAR EARLIER

Ten-year-old Clara hurried down the stairs, struggling with three-year-old Sara in her arms. After reaching the bottom, the two rushed through the front door with a 'wham' and headed toward the barn. Clara struggled slightly due to Sara's weight, but she refused to rest or to put down the child until they got through the open barn door. Once inside, she could see that sixteen-year-old Benjamin and fifteen-year-old Jason were playing in the hayloft. The boys were taking turns jumping from the platform of the second-story loft into the enormous pile of hay below.

"Can I try it?" Clara asked somewhat apprehensively.

"Sure, if you're not a fraidy-cat." It was Benjamin who responded.

Clara sat Sara on the ground next to the barn cat—a creature that thrived on any kind of attention, even from a three-year-old. Sara's tiny hands began to pull on tuffs of cat fur, while the cat purred in response. A few minutes later, Clara was up in the loft where her brothers had been and Benjamin and Jason were down on the first floor (each on either side of the hay pile), encouraging their sister to jump. Meanwhile, thirteen-year-old Emily spied on the entire happening, peering around the barn's door. To be sure, Annabelle was clutched in her arm the entire time.

It was Jason who finally yelled up to his sister: "Come on, Clara, jump! We don't have all day."

Clara looked nervously at the hay pile below her, bent her knees forward to make the jump, and then changed her mind.

"Jump, or I'm going to come up there and push you down!" It was Benjamin who spoke.

Knowing that her older brother would do just that, she bent her knees forward, took a tiny jump and let out a joyful shout as she landed on the soft hay below. When she stood up, she was smiling from ear to ear. She brushed herself off while pleading with her brothers: "Can I do it again? Can I?"

Benjamin grinned back at her, "Okay, once more, then we got to get busy putting this hay up into the loft."

Clara bobbed her head with excitement. She scurried over to the ladder, hurried up to the second floor loft, and this time, without hesitation, jumped off the platform and landed squarely in the middle of the hay pile below. When she reached the ground below, she brushed herself more thoroughly, and went to take Sara's hand, helping the child to her feet.

"I wanna play with Kitty meow," Sara said happily.

"We'll play with the cat some more later," Clara said, just as Emily entered the barn looking at Clara with disgust.

"You're a tom-boy," Emily branded her.

Clara made a face in return, "At least I'm not a fraidy-cat."

Emily smiled as she remembered what she had come for: "Mama wants you," was all that she said.

"What for?"

"It's your turn to do the dishes. Mama told me to watch Sara."

Emily reached out to take Sara by the hand, still clutching Annabelle with her other arm. Clara winced with disgust, stomped her feet and headed back toward the house. Although dreading the prospect of dishes, she knew better than to disobey.

When Clara reached the house, letting the door slam behind her, she first looked at her mother preparing a pie for dinner at one end of the counter and then looked at the washtub next to the sink.

"It's your turn to do the dishes, Clara."

"Yes, Mama." Clara agreed, but she shook her head in dismay, looking at the enormous stack of unwashed plates and pans that stood next to the washtub. The sight made her grimace; it always seemed as though the pile of dishes was the highest when it came her turn to do the wash. She sighed, took one of the dirty plates, and began the task that lay before her.

HUNTSVILLE, UTAH—SUMMER, EARLY AFTERNOON, 2006

"You know, the one chore I just hated was those damn dishes," Clara said as much to herself as to the reporter. "Washing dishes then was a whole lot different than washing them now. You didn't have a machine, or running water, or powders or boxed soap or whatnot. I would have done anything I could to get out of doing dishes but it wasn't something you got out of with Mama."

Clara leaned in Joan's direction and pointed toward the woman's writing tablet. "It might be good if you could let folks know what it was like. We had no such thing as 'Chinet' or paper plates. There was just plain dishes, and they had to be washed after breakfast, after dinner (which today everyone calls lunch), and after supper. You got a big wash tub, and after pumping the water and heating it, you'd have to scrub them down with the lye soap Mama made. Today, folks just flip on their Kenmores and don't give it a second thought . . . The only way I managed to get through it was to standing there with that big wash tub, thinking about Paul."

After making certain that Joan was dutifully taking the notes she had requested, Clara readjusted herself in the chair and began again. "It was a long while before I realized where this whole attraction to Paul came from. By then it was all over anyhow, but it sure made for some fascinating correlation later on."

"Okay, tell me about Paul." Joan sighed, turning a page in her writing tablet, writing the name 'Paul', and underlining it twice.

Clara nodded, "It might be best to talk about the start of this whole attraction—way back, before I had even come into the earth as Clara Stuart."

Joan frowned but decided to say nothing. Clara took a sip of the iced tea that had replaced the pitcher of lemonade and added matter-of-factly: "At the time, he had been an English Lord—went by the name of Lord Clemson."

Joan interrupted, "I though you said he was a trapper by the name of Pete?"

"No, no, no," Clara exclaimed, waving her hand from side to side, "I'm talking about before that. Before the Fort Laramie days, he was Lord Clemson in England. I worked in the kitchen and went by the name of Betsy."

Joan Stuart rolled her eyes and stopped writing; however, the recorder continued to tape the conversation, and Clara Cabot sat back in her chair, closed her eyelids, and pictured the images that had once stood before her:

"His world was far apart from mine. You see, there was this business of class and status and whatnot . . .

and here I was two levels below the housekeeper. A person like myself had no business speaking to Lords and Ladies. If you were spoken to at all, you could respond with, 'Yes'm, me Lord' or 'Yes'm, me Lady' that was the extent of your conversation. I was putting myself in a serious predicament that day by looking in the ballroom, let alone imagining what it would be like being with this man. But when I saw him, well, something happened . . . this business of glands acting up was entirely new to me. And, when it happened I couldn't help my feelings.

"I remember seeing all these beautiful people dancing. They danced in lines or in circles, exchanging couples as the music went along. The dance of the day was the cotillion or contradancing, which usually involved a lot of movements of the feet, hands, and arms, in time with the music; you see, this was more than 100 years before the waltz, and couples holding one another just wouldn't have been proper."

Clara paused and was quiet for a moment before adding as an after-thought, "By the way, Emily was there, too."

LONDON, ENGLAND–GRAND BALLROOM, 1694

A beautiful seventeenth century English ballroom played host to a grand ball, as lords and ladies attended, all dressed in their finery. Throughout the

The Reincarnation of Clara 93

ballroom, a series of four couples created their own double circles as they danced in time to the music. Each individual turned first to the left and then to the right, gently clapping their hands in time with the steps and the rhythm of the music. In the center of the room, a stringed orchestra kept pace with the aristocracy. In fact, some members of the band appeared quite similar to individuals who would one day play instruments at Fort Laramie, and even later in Shorty Ross' Berthana. A perfectly attired twenty-seven-year old Lord Clemson stood across the circle from his partner, Lady Katherine (a woman who would return to Clara's twentieth century schooldays as Gladys Hooper). Together, Lord Clemson and Lady Katherine made one of the most attractive couples in the entire room.

At the far end of the ballroom, the door leading to the kitchen was slightly ajar. Peering through the doorway, a twenty-four-year-old scullery maid named Betsy stared at Lord Clemson as though she was totally enamored. She had been standing and staring for quite some time—never having seen anyone as attractive as Lord Clemson, and never having felt so drawn to another man the way she felt drawn to this handsome lord. However, in the midst of her fantasy, the kitchen's head cook (who would follow Betsy into the twentieth century as her sister Emily) was horrified to see that a young female had left her station of employment and was peering into the ballroom—a place that the young woman was forbidden to venture.

"Missy!" Head Cook/Emily was appalled and quickly grabbed Betsy/Clara by the shoulder, pulling her back into the kitchen and away from the door. "Don't you be gettin' ahead of yourself in my kitchen or they'll be bloody 'ell to pay!"

"Yes'm, Ma'am," the scullery maid replied submissively.

"Now get back to scrubbin' them pots!"

She pushed the younger woman in the direction of an enormous countertop heaped with piles of copper pots and pans. Large tubs for washing and rinsing were stacked side-by-side. Quickly, so as not to incur additional wrath, Betsy got back to work. The Head Cook watched until she was confident that the scullery maid had resumed her duties. The kitchen staff of about a dozen others, scurried about the room making preparations for dessert. As soon as any plate, pot or pan was dirtied, it was thrown in Betsy's evergrowing pile. In an effort to deal with all the work that lay before her, however, the scullery maid simply imagined that it was she who was out on the dance floor, circling with Lord Clemson in time with the music.

Suddenly a large commotion in the pantry brought Betsy back to her task, while members of the kitchen staff gathered around one of the lesser cook helpers (who would be reborn in 1921 as Katie Abbott). The young woman appeared extremely frightened; her eyes were opened wide with terror. She turned from the others and spoke to the head cook:

"I felt it, mum. I felt it as sure as I'm standing here, I did."

The Head Cook was alarmed, "Did you see it?"

The very idea made the young woman shiver with fright, "No, mum. But I felt it for sure; the ghost is back, but I don't want to be seeing it. No, mum!"

The Head Cook lowered her voice, "Where is it?"

"In the pantry, mum, but don't make me go back in there. Please don't make me go in there, mum!"

HUNTSVILLE, UTAH—SUMMER, EARLY AFTERNOON, 2006

Joan couldn't help but interrupt Clara in the midst of the story. "A ghost?" The question was asked with disbelief.

"Oh yes," Clara was positive. "Just like the time when I saw little Sara out feeding the ducks. Same type of thing. I don't think any of the others really saw it, but it had a way of making its presence known if folks ignored it for too long. I saw it myself . . . can't say that I was surprised by it and I certainly wasn't scared like the others. After all, Joanie, it was just a ghost."

"What was it doing there?" She was still skeptical.

"Working in the kitchen. Poor soul didn't know that she was dead."

"What?!"

Clara chuckled, "Now I'm certain the folks down at the Tribune don't want to be hearing this. Let's try to stay on the subject at hand. Let's see, Huntsville just after the war . . . " Clara resumed her rocking motion and pondered the subject before resuming her narration:

"I couldn't get a job in the sewing factory 'cause I had a hard time threading the needle let alone making a pleat. I finally managed to get a job there at the Emporium Theatre over on Main Street. I just loved working there. People were so nice, and everyone dressed up a bit to go out to the show. Usually I had to work behind the refreshment counter but once a week was my night in the ticket booth. I just loved lookin' at what people were wearing. Emily was earning a good bit more money than I was but I don't think she enjoyed herself near as much. I loved the movies almost as much as I loved dancing. Not everyone had TV and the only thing worth watching was Berle's Texaco Star Theatre. You know, you didn't need a channel changer back then, 'cause there was no channels to be flipp'n to. Everyone came to the movies.

"I must have seen Road to Rio thirty times my last year at the Emporium. It was just before Joe and I were married—we had to wait because divorce was drawn out back then. I don't care how many times I saw it, but every time Bob Hope put on that Carmen

Miranda hat and strutted across the plaza with Bing Crosby, well . . . I nearly fell out of my seat. It was the box office champ that year—I heard it made over $4 million dollars. Imagine!

"I loved the Emporium but had to quit soon after we were married. See, it wasn't really proper for a wife to keep working if her husband could support the family. Besides, Joe and I were planning to have children. We were all set to have a family of our own.

"Lord, how the two of us wanted to have a child."

SIX

HUNTSVILLE, UTAH—
DOCTOR'S OFFICE, 1954

Thirty-seven-year-old Joe Cabot and his thirty-three-year-old wife, Clara, were in the doctor's office, sitting across from his desk. The doctor sat in his chair, appearing hesitant to begin the conversation. Several diplomas adorned the paneled wall behind him, along with a framed letter that contained the silhouette of the Mormon Temple in its letterhead. It appeared to be some kind of a thank you or a citation signed by none other than David O. McKay, Mormon Church president. Clara's first thought was that she hadn't even known Dr. Benson was Mormon, but her second thought was that most everyone in the state of Utah was a Mormon.

"I'm really sorry," Dr. Benson began finally, after glancing at the papers on top of the file in front of him. "Usually, we say that couples who have been unable to conceive in the first year or so may have a problem with conception, and the two of you have been trying for three . . . "

"Four," Clara corrected.

Dr. Benson nodded. "Certainly you can keep trying, but I don't want you to get your hopes up. Have the two of you considered adoption? There's a couple in my Ward that adopted, and the two of them couldn't be happier. I'd be delighted to introduce the four of you if you'd like to talk to someone about it."

"Well, we've talked about it," Joe responded when his wife did not. "But I don't know whether or not it's something we're going to pursue."

"I don't want to put additional pressure on the two of you, but if you are contemplating adoption you need to move forward on it in the next year or so. Most agencies consider anyone past the age of 35 as being almost too old, and they'll never consider adopting a child to a woman over forty."

"Do you know what the problem is doctor?" It was Joe who inquired.

"Well, we'd have to pursue more tests, some of which you'd have to be referred to Salt Lake for, as they're beyond the scope of my practice, but to tell you the truth, I don't think I've personally seen a case like the two of yours. Usually it's either the husband *or* the wife who is having problems with infertility . . . "

"Neither one of us can have children," Clara interrupted.

"It appears so, Clara."

Later in the day, Clara and Joe stood at their porch railing staring beyond the "Huntsville Air Force Base" and "No Trespassing" signs at the activity on the base. There was a lull in the sound of jet engines, which often occurred around lunch time. Joe held Clara's hand in his left hand and his cane in his right. Ironically, he couldn't help but think about how much open space they had around them—perfect for children.

Clara finally spoke. "I can't help it, Joe, I always wanted a family."

"We can always adopt, darlin'."

"Joe, for many people that is a wonderful answer, but not for you and me. Don't you think there's a reason we both can't have kids?" she asked, emphasizing the word.

"Fort Laramie's got us both again," he said, shaking his head.

"It's time we fulfilled what once went wrong." She turned him toward her, kissed him firmly on the mouth before giving him a hug. "At least we can go through this together, and at least we have the awareness of what brought this about. You know most people don't have a clue what they've done to create the situations they've been dealt."

"If it wasn't for you, darlin', I'd probably be as 'out to lunch' as the rest of them. I only know these things because I have you in my life."

"Joe, if you didn't already possess the awareness inside yourself, you wouldn't believe half the things I say."

"I better believe them or you'd nag me until I gave in," he said teasingly.

"Oh that's not true, Joe Cabot. My first husband was much dumber than you could ever hope to be, and I could probably count the times I nagged him on one hand."

"One broken hand," came Joe's reply.

"That's in the past," she said, quickly brushing the thought of Paul aside. "Still, isn't it ironic that here we are in the state of Zion, Mormon country, where not having children is something you just don't do? Everybody has children. You know, I was at the Wangsgard's yesterday waiting my turn, and the woman in front of me took out her wallet and showed me this house-full of kids . . . and Joe, all I had was this little picture of you. I felt so ashamed for not having kids."

"There's nothing to be ashamed of, Clara," Joe said softly. "There's nothing to be ashamed of."

He stopped speaking and Clara could see that his eyes were becoming moist. It was clear that Joe had wanted a child as much as she had; it was also clear that there was nothing either one of them could do to get what they really wanted.

HUNTSVILLE, UTAH—SUMMER, EARLY AFTERNOON, 2006

Clara wiped her eyes and looked over at her niece: "Even as a grown woman I used to sit out on this porch before Joe got home from work and remember little Sara and our tea parties, and how I'd help her feed the ducks. Lord, how I missed that child. A few times I even caught myself thinking about that kitten Mama dragged out from under the bed and how I used to hold it, and feed it with a bottle out by the barn so that Emily wouldn't have nothing to be snitching on. I tell you, depression can sure take a person's mind off of the wondrous things they have to be thankful for. I spent about six months feeling sorry for myself. Much of that time I thought about the past there in Samaria City. Sometimes I thought about little Sara, sometimes I thought about Emily, sometimes I even thought about how those other girls always made fun of me.

"I don't know why I was never really comfortable in school. Mama used to say I was too sensitive for my own good—maybe that was it. It was so hard for me to talk to the other kids. I wanted friends but I just didn't know what to say. I ended up sticking out all the more just by keeping to myself." She chuckled, "Who'd have ever thought a day would come when I could hardly keep myself quiet?"

"What do you remember about Paul? I mean, what do you remember from Samaria City?" Joan quickly added.

"It's funny," Clara reflected aloud, "I can remember the first time I saw Paul just as clearly as the day it happened. I remember so many of the times I watched him there in school and the expressions he had on his face, even the clothes he liked to wear. But somehow I have a very difficult time recalling parts of our marriage. Those six years seem kind of fuzzy . . . as if everything ran together and spilled over on itself. All I know is that the eight years I spent imagining what it would be like to be with this boy were worlds apart from what I experienced later on."

"Tell me about the first time you saw him."

"It was the first day of school. This was the Depression and fifth through eight grades were in the same class. We had rows of windows along one wall, which sometimes caused the morning sun to interfere with what you were trying to write on your desk. I remember looking up from my desk at the moment Paul Gabriel took his seat. The sun shone behind his face with such a glare that it was blinding. Suddenly, everything stopped. The room was quiet and I found myself staring. I just couldn't bring myself to turn away. It was quite a shock for a ten-year-old to feel that kind of attraction.

"It would have broken my heart to realize it would

be another five years before Paul said two words to me. But I didn't have a clue. Fifteen years later I could have looked sideways at that boy and got to the heart of this whole connection but I was only ten and didn't even know what past lives were, let alone the fact that I'd been dancing through history with this soul. So there I was, a child sitting next to a thirteen-year-old boy who would soon forget that I was even alive. It didn't make any difference to me. All I knew from that moment on was that I was totally and helplessly in love."

"Do you remember what Paul was like as a boy?"

"Absolutely, I remember. Paul was used to getting his own way. I don't know that you could call him a bully—I certainly didn't think of him in that way but you didn't cross him. He had this air of authority that made it very clear he was the boss. He was so self-assured. In fact, even as a child I realized this boy seemed to think he was just a little better than everybody else. Being so uneasy around others myself, I guess I was attracted to his sense of confidence. His home situation and upbringing were quite different from my own. Both his parents were known to drink, which made for quite a bit a gossip among Mormons and Baptists alike. Later, Mama and Papa forbade me to see him because Paul came from the 'other side of the tracks,' so to speak. Yes, he was very different than I was in so many ways."

Clara Cabot rocked back and forth while Joan

Stuart took down a few notes. When she had finished with the notes, she made sure that the recorder still had room on the tape. At that moment, Clara thought of something that had long been overlooked:

"You know, Joanie? I have never thought about this until this very moment, but all the times I was depressed over not being able to have children, or a little upset about something that had happened to me or to Joe, I would think about other things that had made me depressed. I guess that's pretty normal. But in all those times, never once did I think about Paul Gabriel. I honestly think my marriage to that man was the worst six years of my life. Maybe the fact that I've never given him a second thought is proof that I've finally gotten Lord Clemson out of my system."

SAMARIA CITY, UTAH—CLARA'S CHILDHOOD SCHOOL, SEPTEMBER, 1931

It was a beautiful, sunny day, and the first day of a new school year. Thirty-some students gradually took their seats in the classroom, which had been designated for the fifth through eighth grades. Because the four grades were held together, the students' ages ranged from ten to thirteen. Among the ten-year-olds was an extremely shy Clara Stuart, who took a seat in the back row—one row over from the windows.

The row of windows along the outer wall was

ablaze with the morning sun. The light illuminated ten-year-old Clara's desktop as she sat silently and doodled on a notepad, drawing pictures of cats. The young girl seems oblivious to the other students as they entered and took their seats. Although some of the others seem to be talking in pairs of two or three or at least saying something when another student sat next to them, Clara maintained her silence and spoke to no one.

Although Emily was thirteen-years-old and by age would have been in the same class, Clara's elder sister had skipped a year and was in the ninth grade, taking classes in the same room as fifteen-year-old Jason, who was in the tenth grade, and sixteen-year-old Benjamin, who was in the eleventh. Once again, Clara found herself in a situation in which she was all by herself.

The last student to enter the room was thirteen-year-old Paul Gabriel who appeared quite handsome and older than his years. He took the final seat available—the one on the back row against the outer wall—the one that took most of the direct sunlight. It was also the chair next to Clara. As Clara glanced over to see who was sitting beside her, she was nearly blinded by the sun and by the image of the boy she saw. All at once, Paul became aware that there was a ten-year-old girl staring straight at him:

"Do I know you?" Paul Gabriel asked, appearing somewhat confused.

Clara was instantly embarrassed. The boy had the brightest blue eyes she had ever seen. She quickly shook her head, "No," to which Paul shrugged his shoulders and turned back toward the front of the room. For the rest of the morning, Clara stole glances of the boy out of the corner of her eyes and tried to imagine that she had said something witty in response to his question.

Later that afternoon, when the entire class had been let out on the playground for recess, Clara stood against the brick schoolhouse waiting uncomfortably for the period to end. After all, it was much easier to sit in class and listen to a teacher or to sit and do assignments than it was to wait all by yourself having no one to talk to. She looked around to see if her siblings had been let out for recess but there was generally only a fifteen minute overlap, so as to not have too many students out at any one time. Her brothers or sister were nowhere to be found.

While she was looking for signs of another Stuart, Clara noticed that Paul Gabriel seemed to be speaking awfully loudly to another one of the boys. She just couldn't take her eyes off of the Gabriel boy. Suddenly, Paul pushed the other student as a means of provoking the boy into taking the first swing. Paul got what he wanted, and as soon as the boy swung, Paul swung back and the fight was on. All at once a group of students stood cheering around the two, trying to provoke both boys. It wasn't until the two male students were on top of each other, wrestling on the ground that Mr. Burnett, the gym teacher, ran towards the commotion.

FORT LARAMIE, WYOMING—FORT ENCLOSURE, SEPTEMBER, 1852

Years later an elderly Clara Cabot stood as an unseen silhouette, watching a fight scene in the streets of Fort Laramie between a soldier and twenty-seven-year-old trapper, Pete/Paul Gabriel. A small crowd of cowboys, soldiers, and barmaids (including Clara's twenty-four-year-old counterpart, Esther) had gathered on the wooden porch of the saloon to watch. Reverend Vaux/Everett Stuart passed by the two, obviously disgusted by the scene.

As Clara Cabot watched, the fight between the two boys at school was brought back to mind and she knew beyond any question that the fight she had witnessed as a ten-year-old girl was simply a continuation of the same confrontation she now stood before. Even the Fort's Commander Evans had been there as Mr. Burnett.

Commander Evans/Mr. Burnett ran into the street and fired a gun into the air. The sound forced the soldier and Pete to stop fighting, but the way the two glared at one another made it very clear to all those nearby that the argument between them was far from settled.

FORT LARAMIE, WYOMING—BORDELLO ROOM, THREE DAYS LATER, 1852

Esther/Clara sat on the edge of her bed in her room, staring into the mirror. She had been holding the baby girl, rocking the child gently in her arms until the baby was asleep. Although the child was now sleeping, Esther continued her rocking motion. The dark rings under her eyes suggested that she had been crying, or keeping long hours, or both. Suddenly, there was a knock at her door.

"Russ?" Esther asked expectantly, before changing her mind. "Come in, Mary."

The door cracked open to show the somber face of Mary/Mabel Stuart; she was carrying a tray with a bowl of stew and a glass of sarsaparilla.

"How did you know it was me, honey? I brought you some buffalo stew and a sa'sprilla . . . whiskey's not good for the baby's milk."

"Thanks, Mary. I'm not real hungry right now."

Mary only nodded before placing the tray on top of the dresser. She walked over and sat on the bed next to Esther.

"I'm worried about you, girl."

"Me too."

Mary changed the subject. "One of the fella's been askin' 'bout you."

"Who?"

"That trapper by the name of Pete—he's the one

The Reincarnation of Clara

that gets into a scrape with one of the Commander's boys now and then; nice lookin' fella, though Olive did tell me once that he tended to be a little rough."

"I know who he is . . . what does he want?"

Mary laughed. "What the hell do you think he wants? Apparently, he was at the bar and told Harold he'd give you a $10 Liberty piece just for the afternoon."

"He's about nine months too late."

"I'm serious, Esther, I think this boy likes you."

"I can't see him now." The baby yawned and let out a soft cry, so Esther resumed her rocking. "I would have given him what he wants a couple of years ago, but I can't be doing that to Russ."

"Honey, you can't keep waiting on Russell."

"I'm going to get Russell—I know that for a fact. I don't care what it takes; I'm gonna get him."

With her words, the baby began to cry.

HUNTSVILLE, UTAH—SUMMER, EARLY AFTERNOON, 2006

"Human nature does not change very quickly," Clara Cabot assured her niece. "Most of us pick up right where we left off. Too often, we find ourselves reacting to the shadows of the past, rather than using the free will given to us to choose a better path." Suddenly, Clara chuckled, "No wonder we love reruns."

"Those old patterns are what created a rift between

Emily and I. You just can't imagine how long the two of us had been arguing. Some of those patterns were the root cause of what you might call my issue with self-esteem. Who'd ever think I once had a problem with self-esteem? Imagine! And of course, don't forget that whole issue with Paul. That was a pattern of desire from the past that wasn't easy to shake . . . "

"Did you ever see Paul Gabriel outside of school?"

"Absolutely. I remember the first time very clearly. It was several weeks later that fall but it was unusually warm, which made it a perfect opportunity for Papa to take us all into Samaria City. Once in awhile when there wasn't something pressing at the farm, Papa'd bring us all into town. We could have our choice of a soda, a sundae, or an ice cream cone there at Hurley's store. I used to put myself through fits trying to figure out which one I was gonna have. Today, I'd order one of each and not give it a second thought, but money was scarce. Papa used to trade the Hurley's some of our eggs for the ice cream."

"Actually, I think Sara and I were always the most excited about getting ice cream. Emily was never as interested in ice cream as she was boys—not that she had much luck—but early on both she and Jason had become interested in the 'opposite sex.' You know, I don't think Mama cared much for this business of glands acting up and all . . . no, it was me and Sara who were the most interested.

"I can still see little Sara sitting there at Hurley's

counter that day. Even though Benjamin had adjusted her stool, I think her eyes just barely came up over the counter. Even though I can see her sitting there, I don't remember much of what she said to me that day. Years later I would have given anything just to hear the sound of that little voice. For that reason, I often looked sideways on the day just to reexperience it myself. At the time, I was too caught up in this fantasy about Paul . . . Paul Gabriel, even his name made me think he was an angel. The sun rose and set with his image in my mind. Let me tell you, that kind of attraction was hard for a ten-year-old. My whole life had suddenly been taken over with thoughts of this boy—thoughts I wasn't old enough to understand let alone know where they came from."

SAMARIA CITY, IDAHO—MAIN STREET, OCTOBER, 1931

In the 1930s, Samaria City was a small but bustling town. There was a grocer, a saloon, a barber, a hotel, a Sinclair service station, a Mormon church (Ward), a Baptist church, and a half-dozen other 1920s buildings, including a small train station—all built along a dirt Main Street lined with wooden sidewalks. Although it was October, it was definitely Indian summer, as no one walking Samaria City's streets was wearing a jacket. In addition to the townspeople who walked, quite a number headed down Main Street on bicycles, or in carts, buggies, or surreys. Samaria City had as many horses as it did cars.

The sound of the train whistle blew just as Everett Stuart's old Model-T pulled up to the Hurley's general store and parked behind a beautiful 1929 Graham-Paige automobile. The entire Stuart family had come into town for the afternoon: Clara's mother and father, sixteen-year-old Benjamin, fifteen-year-old Jason, thirteen-year-old Emily, ten-year-old Clara, and three-year-old Sara. Grandfather Stuart had stayed behind for a nap.

Clara helped Sara out of the car, while Benjamin went and joined some of the town's boys gathering around the Graham-Paige. Some of the boys "ooohed" and "aawed" and pointed. Everett Stuart carried a basket of eggs, while Mabel tried to keep track of each of her children. While Benjamin checked out the car, Jason went out of his way to walk near a couple of girls who giggled as he spoke, "Afternoon, ladies." After getting out of the Model T, Emily repeatedly brushed herself off until one of the boys on the wooden sidewalk began to stare in her direction. Clara and Sara were discussing the treat each planned to have, with Clara doing most of the talking.

"Stuart children, come!" Mabel Stuart finally said with that powerful voice that often found expression in the choir.

Benjamin was the first to follow his father into the Hurley's General Store, followed by Emily. Mabel

The Reincarnation of Clara

waited patiently in the door for her other three children.

"Ice cream! Ice cream!" Sara said excitedly.

Clara wondered aloud, "I wonder if Papa will let me have two scoops?"

Jason stood with the two giggling neighbor girls and asked, "What are you ladies doin' out on a fine afternoon like this?"

Finally Mabel had had enough, "Jason, Clara, Sara . . . I'm waiting."

"Yes'm, Mama," Clara responded, bringing Sara in by the hand.

Jason winked at the neighbor girls and then followed obediently behind his sisters.

Hurley's General Store was relatively large and filled with groceries, fruits, vegetables, and dry goods of every description. Mr. Hurley stood up front by the register, ringing up purchases for one of his customers. On the left side of the store was a soda counter with a dozen stools. Behind the counter a plump Mrs. Hurley stood, appearing to wait impatiently for the Stuart family to come in and take their seats. Much of the counter was lined with jars of hard candy, peppermint, and assorted sweets—all of which drew Clara's attention.

Fourteen-year-old Paul Gabriel and a friend were seated at one end of the soda counter but Clara was so caught up in the candy and the possibility of ice cream that Clara didn't even notice. Members of the

Stuart family each took a seat: Emily, Everett, Benjamin, Mabel, Clara, Sara, and finally Jason. Paul was seated several seats down on Jason's right.

Clara turned to her three-year-old sister and repeated a question for the twentieth time, "Do you want some ice cream?"

Sara nodded excitedly. Clara smiled at her sister and then looked over at Jason. She was going to ask Jason what he was thinking of ordering when she spotted Paul. She was so surprised by his appearance that even the thought of ice cream went completely out of her head; all she could do was sit silently and stare, and stare.

Sara looked up at Clara and repeated, "Ice cream." When her sister gave no reply, she tugged on Clara's blouse and repeated, "Ice cream." Still Clara continued to stare in Paul's direction.

It was Jason who turned to see Clara staring at something. He swung his head to the right to see what she was so focused upon, looked back and forth a couple of times, and began to grin. Meanwhile, Mrs. Hurley had already taken the first three Stuart orders.

Jason began to say his sister's name in a soft, sing-songy kind of voice, "Clara . . . Clara . . . "

Clara remained oblivious to him, so Jason repeated, "Clara . . . Clara . . . "

Jason continued to look back and forth, and still Clara kept Paul in her gaze. Jason started to mock her. "Clara . . . Clara, I know a secret. I know a secret."

Just then, Mabel Stuart turned to see what her youngest son was up to.

"I know a secret. I know a secret."

Finally, Clara came to her senses and looked at her brother with shock, "What?"

Jason smiled and continued to sing, "Clara's got a boyfriend . . . Clara's got a boyfriend."

Clara was horrified and immediately became pale just as Mabel Stuart said, "Jason!" and Mrs. Hurley wearily asked Clara, "What would you like to have?"

Clara was shocked, like a wild animal staring into the headlights of an oncoming car and was unable to respond to Mrs. Hurley's question. Finally, it was Sara who looked up and replied, "Ice cweam, please." Only then did Clara finally manage to order a sundae.

Mrs. Hurley skillfully prepared the orders: a cherry coke, several ice cream sodas, a sundae and a couple of dishes of ice cream—each served with a heap of whipped cream and a cherry. After the Stuart family had received their orders, Emily discussed something with her father, and Benjamin repeatedly swung around on his swivel-seat (ice cream in hand) staring through the windows at the new automobile. Jason turned around on his own stool and smiled at a brown-haired teenage girl who had just entered the store with her mother. Sara appeared to be talking incessantly to Clara, but Clara remained totally oblivious to the conversation. Out of the corners of her eyes, she couldn't help but stare at Paul.

LONDON, ENGLAND–ENGLISH MANOR HOUSE KITCHEN, 1694

The scullery maid, Betsy/Clara, stood dreamily in front of her massive pile of dishes. She repeatedly took the same pot, washed it over and over again, and remained completely oblivious to what she was doing because of the daydream that danced through her mind. In her mind, she and Lord Clemson were dancing with another couple, spinning in time with the music. The ballroom music continued to play, while many of the other lords and ladies drank from their goblets, had a bite to eat, or stared in admiration at the attractive figures of Lord Clemson and herself dancing.

While Betsy fantasized and repeatedly washed the same pot, a few of the other kitchen helpers had stopped to watch, and laugh, and Head Cook/Emily began to tap her foot with irritation before screaming aloud:

"Missy!" she said, shaking Betsy by the shoulder. "What in bloody 'ell's wrong with you?"

Betsy immediately sat down the copper pot, "Ma'am?"

"Is there something wrong with you?"

"No, ma'am."

The rest of the kitchen staff stopped working, as all eyes turned to see what was happening between the two.

The Reincarnation of Clara 119

The Head Cook was disgusted. "Just fetch me some flour out of me pantry."

The mere mention of the pantry caused the young cook's helper to shudder with fright. Betsy, however, agreed with the request, "Yes'm, ma'am." She curtsied to the Head Cook, dried her hands upon her apron, and walked into the enormous pantry.

At first, Betsy looked around the room and could see nothing unusual. A large wooden table was in the center of the room, equipped with flour, sugar, and assorted condiments. When she could see nothing out of the ordinary, Betsy squinted her eyes and focused her concentration. Gradually, the form of an elderly transparent woman dressed as a seventeenth century servant came into focus. Obviously, it was the ghost that had caused everyone such fright.

The ghost servant was busily preparing a transparent pie on the wooden table. After materializing completely, the ghost looked up at Betsy and then back at the pie she was making.

"That other young 'un's a queer sort 'a duck, not the least bit friendly is she?"

Betsy nodded in agreement.

"Dearie, as long as you're here, be a love and fetch me that cinnamon there behind ye." The ghost pointed to a large container of cinnamon behind the scullery maid. Betsy nodded and brought the container to the table. The ghost took a transparent spoon, dipped it into the cinnamon, and sprinkled a healthy portion of transparent cinnamon on top of the transparent pie.

Betsy watched what the ghost was doing—not being the least bit afraid. Meanwhile, outside of the pantry Head Cook, the young cook's helper, and several of the others listened with interest, but all they could hear was Betsy's side of the conversation.

"What are you doing?" Betsy inquired.

The ghost appeared exasperated, "Good laws, Dearie, any fool can see I'm makin' a plum pie. I declare the staff is just a wonder to me any more. What with not a 'good day' from any of me fellow servants, and you not even knowing 'bout makin' plum pie. The kitchen's in a bloody shambles it is." The ghost shook her head in disappointment.

"Ma'am, I don't want to frighten you but . . . I think you might be dead. My Momma told me 'bout this sort of thing."

On the other side of the doorway, the Head Cook gasped.

Thinking perhaps that a joke was being played on her, the ghost servant shook her head as she spoke, "If I was dead I don't think I'd be makin' no plum pie for the Master."

The scullery maid tried a different approach, "Are you frightened?"

The question made the woman roll her eyes, "I never been frightened by no plum pie."

"I mean about being dead."

The Reincarnation of Clara 121

The ghost appeared concerned about the young girl's sanity, as she pointed a finger toward her own head and made a circular motion. "Now, missy, you're either a bit touched upstairs or you've got the strangest sense 'bout what a body'll find funny."

"How do you feel?"

"Never better, never better. Had a nasty spell there for awhile, but I haven't felt this good for, well, since . . . "

Betsy suggested, "Forever?"

The ghost was startled. "That's right, dearie. That's right."

"I think you're dead, ma'am."

The woman stopped making the invisible pie and looked Betsy in the eyes. "I always believed when a body died, we'll that was it dearie, that was it."

Betsy shook her head, "I don't think so, ma'am."

"You mean, there's more?"

Betsy shook her head, "Yes."

"And I can stop makin' this plum pie?"

"Yes'm, ma'am."

The ghost servant nodded, removed her transparent apron, wiped her hands with it, and looked around the pantry. "That'll do it then. That'll do it. What comes next, dearie? I'm new to this dying an' all."

"I think you're supposed to look for somebody you know." Betsy pointed just a few feet away to a single line of light that expanded to fill the pantry. Even

Betsy was forced to squint. When the light had engulfed the room, an elderly woman stepped out and reached in the direction of the ghost.

"Grand-mama?" the ghost was surprised but followed after the older woman. Before leaving into the light, however, she turned to Betsy one last time:

"Be a love, Dearie, and give that queer duck a message?"

"Yes'm, ma'am."

"Tell that young 'un it's proper to speak when spoken to."

Suddenly the light and the ghost servant disappeared, as well as the transparent pie and its ingredients. The scullery maid was left by herself, all alone in the pantry.

HUNTSVILLE, UTAH—SUMMER, EARLY AFTERNOON, 2006

Clara rocked matter-of-factly in her chair, as Joan continued writing. When the reporter finally finished, she looked up from what she had been doing and asked her aunt, "So what happens when we die?"

"I looked sideways at that whole question when it was your Uncle Joe's time. I guess it was my way of seeing him off. You get to review your entire life . . . only this time you experience the feelings of all the people you ever encountered and how your actions affected them. Believe me, Joanie, after that experience, you need a good rest."

"Then what?"

"Well, at the very heart of your being, you take stock of who you are. When that's done, it becomes very clear what you need to learn in your next assignment."

"Next assignment?"

"When you're coming back and what it is you'll be attempting to learn."

Joan was not convinced. "What are we trying to learn?"

"To become a better person. We draw to us exactly what we need to become a better person."

She was still doubtful. "So how did Paul Gabriel help you become a better person?"

Clara couldn't help but chuckle, "I used to ask that myself . . . I used to ask that myself. And then it came to me. You see, for such a long time I had looked down on Clara Stuart . . . she was nobody. Today you'd call it a lack of self-esteem. I had to be with someone who thought even less of myself than I did, and in the process I learned to speak up and say, 'You know, Clara's not so bad, after all.'"

"If this is true, Aunt Clara, where is it all headed?"

"Think of the one person you've loved most of all in your entire life, Joanie. When you can feel that same way about every single soul, then you've made it."

"Good God, Clara, we'd have to be like Jesus Christ to do that!"

Clara only smiled and continued rocking. "Exactly, Joanie . . . that's the idea exactly."

SEVEN

HUNTSVILLE, UTAH—
SUMMER AFTERNOON, 2006

Joan looked up from her notes and wondered aloud, "So what did you and Uncle Joe like to do for fun?"

"You mean besides the Berthana, the noodle parlor, the theatre and such? Well, we had lots of things we liked to do. During the summer we'd make three or four trips to Lagoon over in Farmington. Joe loved that old wooden roller coaster, and I was kind of partial to their gardens. If you've ever had the chance to see those gardens about a day or so after a big rain, there's so many flower blooms you almost expect them to hop off the vine.

"The flowers at Temple Square are also a site to

behold!" Clara added enthusiastically. "Joe wasn't much for walking on account of his leg, but we sure liked to sit on one of those benches near the Mormon Temple and just gander at the walkways through the gardens. What always amazed me, Joanie, was the fact that the gardens were always perfectly kept up with not one weed in site, and never once did we see someone working on the grounds—never once! I always liked to think it was some kind of miracle.

"You know, if we made that trip into Salt Lake, we generally had lunch there at the ZCMI department store. It was kind of like a tradition between the two of us. I loved their fish and chips—actually, I use to think that was the only seafood in all of Utah worth eating. Joe liked their soup and sandwich special.

"Your Uncle Joe was also partial to watching ice skating, so quite a number of times we went to the Salt Palace to see an exhibition. Joe would have loved all the hoopla over the Olympics in '02." Clara sighed. "I just wish he would have lived long enough to see it. If we were out late for an exhibition, we generally did something quick like a Dee's hamburger or maybe we'd stop in at the Big Boy.

"Now don't get the idea that we ate out all the time, 'cause that certainly wasn't the case—maybe dinner out a couple of times a month. But if we were going out, more often than not Joe wanted to go over to Maddox Restaurant there in Pleasant View. He just loved their half a chicken and that sweet tea. We'd

The Reincarnation of Clara 127

usually go for an early dinner around 5:00 p.m. for two reasons: by 5:30 there was a line straight out the door and you'd have to wait, and after an early dinner Joe just loved to go over to Pleasant View's hot pots, so he could soak his leg. We'd both take our swimsuits and a towel, and change out of our dinner clothes in the locker rooms there by the pool. Afterwards, we'd meet in those natural hot springs. It was a great way to soak for an hour or so."

"How did Uncle Joe hurt his leg in the first place?" Joan inquired.

"I guess it depends on what you mean by 'in the first place.' He didn't always work as a purchasing agent at the station. For a number of years he worked out in the train yard as a brakeman—that's when he had been involved in an accident. 'Course this was before Emily had gawked at him there in the lobby of the Ambassador Hotel.

"Joe told me he was riding on the back of a train and watching it back up to connect with a line of box cars. Apparently the conductor didn't stop in time or the train was going too fast . . . whatever it was, your Uncle Joe was thrown off of the back of that train and for a brief instant his leg was pinned between the car he had been riding and the box car they were connecting to. Luckily, it just crushed his leg and hurt his back. Doctors didn't think he'd walk again but they pieced his leg back together as best they could. He had to be in a wheelchair for about three months, then a walker. Eventually he could walk with a cane. 'Course his days as a brakeman were over. Southern Pacific gave him some training and the purchasing job after it opened up. The railroad use to take care of its own—it was a great place to work for the longest time.

"But, Joanie, it would be a mistake to think that the train accident was the sole cause of Joe Cabot's leg problem. You'd have to go all the way back to Fort Laramie for that . . . if the truth be known, it was actually Fort Laramie that became the root cause of his leg problem in the first place."

FORT LARAMIE, WYOMING—FORT ENCLOSURE, OCTOBER, 1852

Twenty-six-year-old Esther/Clara was outside of the saloon, sitting by herself on the far end of the porch with her legs dangling over the edge. The baby was finally asleep, upstairs in her room and she needed this time alone with her thoughts.

She had stopped working during the days altogether, and only put in about four hours or so late at night slinging drinks. There wasn't much money coming in—more was going out, just paying for the rent on her room—but Esther wasn't worried about money; she possessed a few skills that could bring in as many bank notes or Liberty gold as was needed. What she needed was to figure out what to do with

The Reincarnation of Clara

the baby, and how to get Russ. Truth was that the baby was the biggest hurdle between them.

Esther knew she had feelings for the infant—after all, she had given birth to a beautiful child. But she hadn't planned to name it yet or get too attached, just in case. It was simply a matter of fact that she could always have another baby. It was a husband that wasn't easy to come by—especially for someone like herself, with her past. She had latched onto Russ and she wasn't easily going to let go.

He was gone for a few days—off on another trapping expedition with some of the others. Generally he worked alone but rumors continued that a couple of bands of Sioux were out for revenge on account of the actions of a handful of military men who had apparently taken the whole matter of Indian affairs into their own hands. She had heard that two Sioux warriors and one Indian squaw had been shot, but Esther had no proof to back the claim. Usually U.S. soldiers simply took their aggression out on a herd of buffalo, leaving carcasses to rot in the sun, but apparently a few officers had instead chosen the Sioux to be their target. In truth, far too many soldiers and settlers alike believed that the entire Indian nation stood in the way of westward migration.

"The Indian and the buffalo were here first!" Esther mumbled her words aloud, although no one else was within hearing distance. More than that, she had met many white men she wouldn't trust in the least but an Indian generally held true to his word.

Just as the thought entered her head, Esther heard the commotion. She turned to see a group of children from the church, along with Reverend Vaux, Commander Evans, the blacksmith, and a few others running into the street to surround a couple of horses. She looked again and realized that two men had been thrown over their horses and were being brought to town by none other than a Sioux, riding horseback. The men were obviously hurt.

"Jesus Christ," she muttered, before pushing herself off of the porch and running in the direction of the commotion. It took her only a moment before she reached Commander Evans, who was speaking Sioux to the Indian.

Esther pushed her way to the front. "What's going on?"

"There's no call for a Jezebel," Reverend Vaux said angrily, as he pointed back in the direction of the saloon.

Esther ignored him, and asked again, "What's going on?" only to have Commander Evans raise his hand for silence. As he continued listening, the blacksmith and several of the fort's soldiers began pulling the two men off their horses and carried them inside the fort's quarters. Both of the men were covered in dirt from head to toe, so that a great cloud of dust was dislodged with the movement. It was impossible to see who they were; instead, Esther waited for the

Sioux to finish speaking so that the Commander could interpret what had happened.

Finally, Commander Evans turned to those who had gathered. "The Indian says there was a stampede—a buffalo stampede. He came across the men too late—after the herd had already passed and done its damage. He thinks one of the men is dead—apparently his chest was crushed by the herd. The other man is unconscious. When the Sioux first found him, he was muttering in quite a bit of pain; the Indian thinks one of his legs is badly broken."

"Who were the men?" one of the other girls called out from the saloon.

"The Indian said it was a couple of trappers."

Esther felt her heart fall into her chest, just as the blacksmith came running out of the fort's lodging, proclaiming for all to hear: "That fellow Pete is dead. The other guy . . . Russell's his name . . . is in pretty bad shape—I think his leg has been crushed."

Esther pushed her way through the street and ran in the direction of the fort.

HUNTSVILLE, UTAH—SUMMER AFTERNOON, 2006

Clara brushed a few crumbs from her lap and made certain that Joanie was still recording before beginning again. "The first time I ever kissed a boy was at my cousin Anna's, over in Malad. Malad wasn't that far from Samaria City but back then it seemed like quite a distance so I only got to see her three or four times a year. She and I were the same age, but she always seemed so much more mature 'cause of being from the city and all. She was used to going to parties, and having outings like 'staying over' at a girlfriend's and so forth. She even knew about this business of 'twirling the bottle', and doing all sorts of things I had never even heard about on the farm.

"I remember Mama being a little nervous every time I went to visit 'cause my cousin seemed to know so much more than I did, and Mama wasn't certain if these were things a young girl ought to be knowing to begin with.

"To tell you the truth, I was really awkward with this game of twirling the bottle and how if the bottle stopped in front of a fellow you were supposed to kiss him. I didn't care for it at all, but I didn't want to be a bad sport so I went along with the game," Clara chuckled. "It just seemed so scary to me at the time—imagine!

"I remember once when I was about thirteen I had been over at Anna's and had the opportunity to see Grandpa Stuart . . . "

"Did he come with you into Malad?" Joan looked up from her writing tablet.

"Heavens no," Clara shook her head. "He had died about two or three months earlier. I think he came just to show me that he was doing all right."

Joan put down her tablet and frowned. "I don't know what to think about all of this, Aunt Clara."

"Just keep writing, Joanie. It gets better." The old woman smiled and reached for her glass of tea.

MALAD, IDAHO—EMPTY GARAGE, SUMMER, 1934

The one car garage was empty, except for an assortment of tools on the walls, a multitude of oil stains on the cement floor, a goodly number of spider webs in the side window, and the laughter of six children sitting in a circle on the floor—three boys and three girls, all between the ages of twelve and fourteen. The garage door had been closed, as it had been decided by the group of six (at least those who had spoken up) that the game of "twirlin' the bottle" was best played without the knowledge or interference of any adult. Anna, whose father owned the garage, was obviously in charge. In the center of the circle was one solitary Coke bottle, lying empty on its side

"Now if you spin and the bottle lands on you or on the same sex as you, you must spin again." Anna spoke from experience. "But if you spin twice and still do not get the opposite sex, you just lose your turn."

Neither Clara nor Liza, the other girl, had ever played before; Clara's eyes seemed filled with nervousness but Liza appeared quite open to kissing any of the three boys in the circle: Harold, Thomas, or Andrew.

"What if we don't want to kiss the girl the bottle lands on?" Harold asked teasingly, but Clara diverted her eyes nonetheless, just in case he had been referring to her.

"That's not an option," Anna said forcefully. "If you're going to play, you've got to play by the rules."

"Let's just spin already," Thomas said impatiently. "I've got other things to do."

"Fine!" Anna gave him a glaring look. "I'll start."

Anna spun the Coke bottle like a pro, for she had often practiced on her own. She watched in fascination as it circled more than twice. She had been hoping that her first spin would land on Thomas but after his comment she had changed her choice to Andrew. When the bottle finally came to a stop, pointing almost exactly at Harold, she leaned over it and gave him a quick kiss right on the lips. After all, a boy was still a boy.

Andrew was next, he spun the bottle with much less skill than his predecessor and frowned when it landed on himself.

"Spin again." Anna urged him. "Spin harder this time."

He spun and the bottle moved in an irregular pattern—hardly a circle at all—before coming to a stop almost exactly between Harold and Liza.

"Kiss Liza," Anna demanded.

Before Andrew could even lean over and plant a kiss, Liza was quickly on her knees and leaning back in his direction, kissing him a split second before he had kissed her.

It was Clara's turn. She appeared nervous and hesitant, causing Anna to speak out: "Just spin it, Clara!"

Clara took a breath, spun the bottle and watched as it completed a full circle and came to a stop just in front of Harold. She and Harold leaned over at about the same time. Clara closed her eyes and the two of them managed a slight peck, almost on the lips. In spite of her nervousness, Clara found herself thinking that for a first kiss it sure wasn't much.

When she opened her eyes, her mouth fell open in surprise. To her astonishment she could see the transparent form of Grandfather Stuart walking through the garage wall and coming to a stop about two feet away from the circle. Clara was startled but appeared delighted nonetheless. Before she had even thought the situation through, she found herself speaking aloud, "Grandpa?"

Several of the children looked at each other in confusion and Anna encouraged them to keep playing: "She's a day-dreamer," came the excuse.

Although transparent, Clara's grandfather was smoking his pipe. He smiled, tipped his hat and winked before speaking words that only Clara could hear: "I've been thinking about you child. I hope you're okay."

Clara nodded, just as Thomas spun the bottle, only to have it stop and point directly at Clara. He leaned forward to be kissed, but Clara was so caught up in this happening with her grandfather that she didn't move. Finally, both Anna and Thomas called out in unison, "Clara!"

Startled, Clara leaned forward for her kiss. However, when she turned back to look in the direction of Grandpa Stuart, he was gone.

Anna just shook her head in disgust. "You are always in your own little world, Clara. Sometimes, I don't know how you manage."

SAMARIA CITY, IDAHO—CLARA'S SCHOOL, FIRST DAY OF FALL SEMESTER, 1935

Fifteen-year-old Clara was sitting on a bench out front of the schoolhouse, pretending to look at her textbook, however, her actual glance was in the direction of eighteen-year-old Paul Gabriel, who was speaking with Gladys Hooper and Katie Abbott. It was obvious that both girls were laughing at whatever came out of Paul's mouth. "Show offs," Clara muttered to herself. Still, Clara was not about to let her self be upset by their shenanigans. After several years of separation due to their age difference, she and Paul were once again in the same class.

At long last, Clara's body has matured over the summer. The shape of her breasts made it quite obvious that she was no longer a child. But more had changed than simply her appearance—Clara had finally gained a little self-confidence. In fact, she had finally looked sideways at the issue of Paul and the certainty that they *would be* together had reassured her that her longstanding infatuation had not been in vain.

The school bell rang, and Paul walked towards the building with Gladys and Katie giggling just two footsteps behind him. He passed by Clara, just as Clara was closing her textbook—trying hard not to look directly at him. Paul looked at her and was about to walk by but he stopped and looked again. Something was very different about Clara. He smiled just as she looked up.

"Hello, Clara," he said, making his voice sound even deeper than Clara remembered it.

Although she was unable to speak, Clara did manage a smile in return. Both Katie and Gladys looked at her with disgust as they passed. Clara looked away, fumbled with her books, and then followed the others inside. As Clara walked through the hallway, a number of students noticed her new look but for the most part she was ignored. She planned to follow Paul all the way to the classroom, picking a seat nearby but instead she nearly ran right square into Emily, who looked at her with a sister's disdain.

"What do you think you're doing?" Emily asked in disgust. "I told you to meet me in class!"

Clara only sighed.

HUNTSVILLE, UTAH—OUTSIDE EMILY'S APARTMENT, 1946

Twenty-five-year-old Clara Stuart, formerly Clara Gabriel, felt guilty. "Guilty as sin," she thought to herself as she walked along Main Street with Joe by her side. They were arm in arm, which seemed the slightest bit indecent for a second date, but she was happy—happy and guilty, just like so much of her Baptist upbringing. Still, it wasn't really fair to Emily—after all, Emily had seen him first, but he hadn't been interested in Emily! Even if Clara hadn't wanted to go out with him, he hadn't planned on going out with Emily. Joe had told her that Emily just wasn't his type. Then why did she feel guilty? Her mind raced back and forth between being happy about Joe and nervous about Emily.

If she wasn't doing anything wrong, then why was she keeping it from Emily? She had lied about having to work at the Emporium, but it was only a little lie. She and Joe *had gone* to the Emporium. But she wasn't working; it was more of a date—it was a real date. Emily was going to be fit to be tied.

"I had a really good time tonight, Clara." Joe said when they finally reached the front door of the Ambassador Hotel. "That was a good movie."

"I just love a William Wyler film." Clara nervously looked up at the windows to see if Emily was watching to the street below. " . . . Although I still think

Wuthering Heights is my favorite."

"I love a good comedy. Did you see Road to Utopia?"

"About thirty times," Clara smiled. "You forget, I work at the Emporium. I heard Hedda Hopper on the radio a couple of weeks ago saying that Hope and Cosby are coming out with another Road picture next year."

"Do you want to go to it?"

"Are you asking me for another date a year from now?"

"Clara, I'd like to ask you out for every date you've got available." Joe Cabot grasped her head between his hands and kissed her first on the forehead and then on the lips—right there in front of the Ambassador, which caused Clara to blush.

"Did I embarrass you?" Joe asked softly.

"I've seen worse," was all she could manage to say. She leaned forward and gave Joe another kiss on the side of the lips, before hurrying into the hotel lobby, hearing Joe call out, "I'll call you tomorrow," just before the door closed.

Clara hurried up to Emily's apartment, stood in front of the door, and took a breath to become calm. She had just finished reassuring herself that Emily still didn't know a thing, when the door swung open.

"What the hell do you think you're doing?" Emily was furious. She grabbed her sister by the arm, pulling Clara inside the apartment. "I saw you with Joe!"

HUNTSVILLE, UTAH—SUMMER AFTERNOON, 2006

"I'm not saying that your Uncle Joe was perfect, and I'm not saying that we never fought," Clara tapped her finger on the tabletop to emphasize the point for her niece, "even the best relationships present more than enough opportunities to argue. I guess that's just part of the way we help each other rub off the rough spots.

"Sometimes it's hard for a widow to remember all the topics of disagreement between herself and her dead husband. I've often heard tell that a widow will 'saint' her deceased husband after a couple of years of being alone until the man she remembers hardly resembles the man that died. I guess it's because the dead make so few mistakes.

"I do remember arguing about this house—Joe really wanted to move after the Air Force base designation and build up, and I insisted we stay put. Even though I had complained about the noise much more often than he did, I wanted to stay. Let me tell you, that made for a number of heated discussions between us. We also had little disagreements about the same things most couple's argue about: money and leaving dirty clothes on the floor and whose turn it is to pick TV, and so forth. We never argued about sex though—your Uncle Joe and I were right in sync when it came to sex.

"Most of the time we really enjoyed each other's company—whether it was seeing a show, going out to dinner, driving over to Ogden Canyon, or just talking. I think being friends with your spouse is the most important part of any relationship. My marriage to Joe was so different than the time I spent with Paul."

"Do you want to talk about being married to Paul?" Joan finally broached the subject.

"I guess if we have to," Clara chuckled. "I guess if we have to." She took a sip of tea and pondered the question, while Joan changed the tape in her machine.

"For the longest time, Paul appeared to be such a catch." Clara began as Joanie turned a page in her writing tablet, wrote 'Paul Gabriel' (for the second time) and underlined it twice. "Girls just gathered around him like flies to honey. For some reason, he seemed rather sophisticated and just took it for granted that any young lady couldn't wait to be his date. It was like a dream come true when the two of us actually got married. I guess the first four months of our marriage went like any other. We learned to adjust to each other: toilet seats up and down, not squeezing the Ipana from the middle of the tube and whatnot. We got a house in Samaria City, and Paul worked as a mechanic at the Sinclair station.

"Emily had already gone off to Huntsville to find a man . . . she came back for the wedding, though," Clara added as an afterthought. "Benjamin and your father were convinced we were on the verge of war because of the European conflict; they enlisted before being called. You know, Paul's asthma kept him out for the duration . . . he felt real bad about that. Eventually he took it out on me.

"Things were pretty normal, before the dark days anyway. Once in awhile Mama and Papa would come into town for supper . . . "

SAMARIA CITY, IDAHO—GABRIEL HOUSEHOLD, SPRING EVENING, 1941

Paul and Clara Gabriel lived in a quaint one-story home on a quiet street, two blocks south of Main. The house was sparsely furnished, due to their newlywed status and their level of income, but they had a used table and four chairs in the living room and were not adverse to a game of Monopoly or a hand of cards, in spite of being Baptists.

A clock on the living room wall pinpointed the time at 9:30 p.m. Mabel and Everett Stuart sat at opposite sides of the table, with most of the Monopoly properties already having been sold. Twenty-year-old Clara sat across from her twenty-three-year-old husband, each focusing upon the game board.

Everett Stuart picked up the few assorted bills that remained in his pile and looked at the properties he had available. He had just landed on a hotel on Marvin's Gardens, which belonged to his wife. He shuffled the currency, looked at the mortgage value

The Reincarnation of Clara

of his property, and shook his head in disgust. After picking up his money for the third time, Mabel Stuart had had enough:

"Everett, if you can't pay the rent, you're out."

Everett frowned but reluctantly agreed. His wife began collecting the few bills he had left, as he was obviously out of the game. With the pressure off, Everett was ready to get back to the conversation:

"Did you hear, the widow Hurley sold the General Store to a Chinaman?"

Paul Gabriel was shocked. "No! Where'd a Chink get that kind of money?"

"Don't know," Everett continued, "I hear he's a pretty industrious sort of fella."

"God damn it." Paul was incensed. All these damn foreigners. The barber's a Limey, Samara's got two families of Niggers, now a Chink. Clara, we gotta get out of here!"

"Oh Paul, people are people."

"Coloreds ain't people."

Clara was patient. "I like to think everybody is some sort of color, Paul. It just depends on what shade of crayola the good Lord was using when he filled us in. People are just people."

"Colored ain't no people!" Paul said angrily.

"Hush, you two," Mabel Stuart said firmly. "I got a game to win."

Paul was not happy about being corrected by his wife or hushed by his mother-in-law. For the rest of the game, he remained quiet. Twenty minutes later, as he stood on his porch with his wife and dutifully watched his in-laws drive off in their 1939 Ford, he grabbed his wife by the arm, pulled her inside the house, and slammed the door.

"Paul, you're hurting me!"

Without a word, he pulled back his hand and slapped Clara firmly across the face. "Don't you *ever* disagree with me in front of your folks again!"

Clara was completely shocked. She stood there and looked at her husband. She rubbed the side of her jaw and continued to look at Paul as though she was totally confused. She did not know what to say or do.

It would be the first of many such interactions between them.

SAMARIA CITY, IDAHO—DOCTOR'S OFFICE, ONE YEAR LATER

Doctor Patrick was Samaria City's only doctor. To be sure, there were three or four other MD's over in Malad, but Doctor Patrick remained the primary caregiver for most of the townspeople. He had just finished rewrapping Clara's lower chest with an ace bandage below her brassiere.

Clara sat quietly in the chair, while the doctor made a few notes on his chart. Paul paced against the wall, looking at his watch.

"Well Clara, it does appear to be healing nicely. It's still a little tender to the touch?" He asked, after looking up from her file.

"A little," Clara replied softly.

"I still don't think I've ever had a patient who broke three ribs from falling out of bed before. Maybe you should get a bed guard?"

Clara said nothing but Paul was quick to agree. "We'll do just that, Doc. I guess that metal sideboard must have hit her just right."

Doctor Patrick remained puzzled and glanced back down at the file. "Didn't you also break your arm last fall?"

Paul answered, "Sometimes she's a real klutz, but you know I love her."

Doctor Patrick frowned, put his hand under Clara's chin and lifted her eyes to see his. "Clara, that about does it but I want you to know, if anything else bothers you, you come in to see me. Do you understand?"

It was Paul who agreed. "We'll do that, Doc; we'll do just that."

HUNTSVILLE, UTAH—SUMMER AFTERNOON, 2006

Clara finished speaking and turned toward Joanie. The younger woman was grimacing, so Clara inquired: "Is the baby moving?"

"It feels more like summersaults, but it's actually

reassuring; at least I know she's okay.

"I haven't been pregnant this time around but I can't imagine it's much of a state fair." Clara smiled as she spoke the familiar words.

"As long as she's moving, it also takes my mind off my back and feet."

Clara nodded before asking: "Are you doing okay, Joanie? I mean really?"

"You mean, am I doing okay as an unwed, pregnant, mother-to-be?"

"Yes, that's what I mean. Is there a chance things could work out with Larry?"

"Larry wouldn't make much of a father. He's pretty much out of the picture."

"What about child support, Joanie? You're going to need some help."

"I'm really not crazy about the idea of having to deal with Larry for another 18 years. Plus, Larry's got a vengeful streak. If I took him to court for child support, I'm sure he'd go for joint custody—just to spite me. I don't want that for my baby."

"Do you want me to see?"

Joan looked perplexed. "To see what?"

"Do you want me to look sideways at that very question?"

"You can do that?"

"You might be surprised at the things you can look sideways at."

"What do I need to do?"

Clara simply readjusted her position, turning in her chair to face her niece. "Just let me stare at you for a moment."

Joan sat silent and didn't move, while Clara took a long, deep breath and watched her niece until multiple images of Joanie appeared one behind another, as though the old woman was seeing cross-eyed. Finally, there was a tremendous flash of light, and Clara's mind moved beyond the confines of the porch.

SALT LAKE CITY, UTAH—LARRY GREELEY'S APARTMENT, SEVEN-AND-A-HALF MONTHS EARLIER

An invisible silhouette of eighty-five-year-old Clara Cabot found herself standing as witness to the shadows of the past. She watched quietly from one corner of the bedroom as the scene unfolded before her—"P Day," as Joanie had called it. The day Larry found out that Joanie was pregnant.

Larry Greeley maintained some of the chiseled good looks of a high school athlete, in spite of the fact that he was 18 months from 30. He pulled his pants back on, brushed his hands through his hair, and turned toward Joan, who was still in his bed. He shrugged his shoulders, looked at his watch, and spoke somewhat sternly as if to emphasize the fact that she wasn't moving fast enough:

"I thought we were going to get something to eat?"

Joanie remained still, sitting with her back up against the headboard, showing her bare breasts. Larry always thought they looked like a pair of headlights on a motorcycle. Joanie frowned back at him. Although it was not what she had been working up the nerve to say, his coldness after just having had sex gave expression to something else that had often been on her mind:

"Larry, where are we going with this?"

"What are you talking about?"

Joan couldn't believe she had to explain it again. "What are we doing as a couple?"

"Oh for shit's sake! Not again! Can't we just have sex and dinner and not worry about it?" Larry shook his head in disgust, but went ahead and put on his shirt.

"Larry, I think we need to talk about this. What are our plans for the future?"

"Why can't we just keep doing what we're doing, without making plans?"

"Because we've been doing it for nearly three-and-a-half years. That's why."

"Joan, we're not even thirty. We don't need to think about settling down."

"I need to think about it."

Larry just shook his head as he sat down to tie his shoes.

Joan was frustrated and disgusted. "Can't we talk about this? Can't you stop getting ready for five

The Reincarnation of Clara

minutes and talk about this?"

"Look, Joan, I'm going to dinner. I'm hungry. If you want to sit here and make plans for the future, fine. I'm just not ready. All I want to do is eat."

She looked him right square in the eyes: "Larry, I'm pregnant."

Although noticeably shocked, his words were immediate: "Oh, for shit's sake! What a way to ruin an evening."

"I think we should talk about this."

"What do you think we should say?"

"We need to talk about the baby?"

"Joan, it's not a baby; it's a fucking zygote. You need to get rid of it so we can get on with our lives."

"This baby is a chance to get on with our lives."

"It isn't a baby; and we're not keeping it. I'm not ready to settle down. You need to have an abortion."

"I'm not having an abortion, Larry. I'm keeping this baby."

"There's no way. We're not getting married and you're not having a baby!"

Larry was looking more and more angry; Joan looked like she was on the verge of crying, but she did not.

"What have I been to you for the last three-and-a-half years?"

"You don't want to go there."

"Tell me."

"You don't want to go there."

"Larry, I want to know."

"You want me to say it, I'll say it. You've been a fuck buddy. It's been worth putting up with you because of the sex, but there's no way I'm getting married. No fucking way!"

"Can't we just talk like normal adults about this? Larry, this is *our* baby."

"Look, you were the one that got yourself pregnant."

"Larry, I am on the pill. Don't you think there could be a reason for this?"

Larry just clenched his fists and looked as if he was about to explode. "I'm going to get something to eat, and I want you and your stuff out of here when I get back. You can send me the bill for the abortion, but I don't want to hear anything else from you." He paced back and forth next to the bed, like he was an animal in some kind of cage before adding: "I think you have to be pretty stupid to get yourself pregnant." With that, he stormed out of the bedroom just as Joanie began to cry.

The invisible Clara Cabot muttered to herself, "My poor dear," and then she saw a tremendous flash of light.

SALT LAKE CITY, UTAH—COURTHOUSE STEPS ACROSS FROM TEMPLE SQUARE, 22 MONTHS LATER, APRIL 2007

Joan Stuart walked up the courthouse steps with her baby girl in her arms and her lawyer by her side. Eighty-five-year-old Clara Cabot was already at the top of the steps, invisible and aware that she was witnessing shadows of things that could be. Larry Greeley was also at the top of the steps speaking to his sympathetic female lawyer. He was dressed in his best suit and tie and appeared confident and cocky about the outcome of the proceedings. Joan hadn't expected to see him outside the courthouse.

"Hello, Joan, how are you?" he said in his phony, friendly attitude that she had seen him use with waiters and waitresses a hundred times before.

"I'm fine."

"By the way, I don't think you met my fiancée, Bridget." Larry said, introducing his lawyer. We'll be seeking full custody, as I'm very, very worried that your erratic schedule with the paper just doesn't provide my daughter with the nurturing environment she needs."

"You'll never get it." Joan was adamant.

It was Bridget who answered. "We will at least get half. She can live with us six months out of the year but you can see her on alternate weekends."

"It will never happen." Joan was firm but less positive.

Larry was smiling, "I can assure you it will happen. You see, Joanie, I've converted to LDS to be the same religion as my fiancée here, and I know our good Mormon judge will understand the importance of the *true faith* being a part of our daughter's upbringing."

Joan turned white and appeared as if she was about to throw up.

"Are you ready to go inside?" Larry took the arm of his lawyer/fiancée and walked toward the court's entrance.

Clara Cabot was disgusted by the whole performance. "You're absolutely right, Joanie," she said, knowing that Joanie could hear her while sitting on the porch from last summer. "Larry is one hell of a bastard."

EIGHT

HUNTSVILLE, UTAH—
SUMMER, LATE AFTERNOON, 2006

"I don't understand young people today," Clara shook her head in wonderment. "Dating back when I was a child was a very different matter . . . there has always been sex, but the majority of us weren't having any. A date was just a date. Why Joanie, if a boy had ever asked me 'my place or yours?' I wouldn't have known what he was talking about. Not that I had many dates, but its just the way things were.

"If a fella asked you out for Saturday night, well all week long you'd be planning on how you were gonna dress, and how you were gonna look, and if a boy held your hand, or gave you a kiss on the cheek when he brought you home, well, that was like going steady. Most times a date was just a trip to the movies, or maybe a little dinner there in town. Those that could went dancing. Sometimes young people would just go for ice cream. Now, when the county fair came to Malad, that was really something.

"I actually had my first date over at the county fair when I was fifteen. His name was Fred, and he wasn't much of a looker, but he was nice. He asked me out one day in school, and I was as surprised as he was nervous. Mama and Papa said I could go, but Mama made me promise we wouldn't be going to the dancing pavilion what with us being Baptists and all.

"What I remember most about Fred was he had these big, thick glasses that kept sliding down his nose and he had to keep pushing 'em back in place. I think Fred became a pharmacist up there in Boise. Other than it being my first date, I remember two things about that day. The fair had a tent with a fat woman in it; you could go in and view her for a nickel. Fred took me inside. Now all she was doing was sittin' there and reading a detective magazine. They had a box of chocolates sitting next to her for effect, but I never saw her eat any. And after you stared at her sitting there reading, well that was about the extent of it.

"The other thing I remember was seeing Paul Gabriel there with Gladys Hooper on the merry-go-round. She was pretending to be frightened about sittin' up on that painted wooden horse, and Paul was having to stand next to her and hold on to her while the merry-go-round made its turns. I couldn't believe what I was seeing . . . even took my mind off Fred and his glasses. Here five and six year-old children were riding painted horses around without any problem, and Gladys Hooper was actin' like such a baby. I was kind of disgusted with the whole thing."

MALAD, IDAHO—COUNTY FAIRGROUND, 1936

The county fair was the biggest event of the year, and it boasted something for everyone. There was a merry-go-round, a Ferris wheel, a rickety old roller coaster about as tall as a two-story house, a wide selection of carnival games, a dance pavilion, and quite a selection of food. There was also a place for people to spread out the blankets they had brought from home and enjoy some food from the fair, a picnic lunch, a cotton candy, or a drink of soda pop.

On the other side of the fair, past the amusements and rides, there were about 40 pens for the judging of livestock and the local 4-H club to present the awards for the prize pig, the prize calf, and the occasional "rare" creature that wasn't normally seen in Malad. Every year, old farmer Hollis would trot out his male peacock—to the "oohs" and "awhs" of some of the schoolchildren—and one year Clara had even seen a box turtle in one of the pens about the size of a homemade pie. She remembered it had a small hole drilled in its shell back by a hind leg with a thin, long chain put through it as a means of giving the creature just enough room to walk without making an escape.

Fifteen-year-old Clara Stuart walked next to Fred Owens, both looking shy and nervous. They had just finished leaving the fat lady's tent, and although Clara hadn't been at all impressed (and she sure wouldn't need to spend a nickel to see the woman again next year) when Fred said: "That was the fattest person I've ever seen," Clara replied, "Yeah, that was interesting." After that, the silence between them felt a little awkward but Clara didn't know what else to say; she sure couldn't ask, "So, Fred, what do you know about Paul Gabriel?"

Finally, Clara managed a question. "Is any of your family coming to the fair, Fred?"

"My brothers will be here." Fred's voice cracked. "But I think my Pa's got work he wants to do around the farm, and I know Ma won't come without him. She does like the fair, but she told me: "There will always be a fair next year."

There was silence before Fred asked: "How about your folks?"

"I don't think so, but I know Jason will be here." She wanted to add, "As long as there is at least one girl at the fair, Jason is bound to be here," but she didn't know Fred Owens that well.

The Reincarnation of Clara

It was okay enough being around Fred Owens, but it sure wasn't much of a date. Clara had just found herself thinking what it would be like to be at the fair with Paul Gabriel when she saw him with none other than Gladys Hooper, on the merry-go-round, right in front of she and Fred. That woman was nothing but "a damn flirt," excuse the language, Clara thought to herself.

Clara heard Fred mutter something about whether or not she wanted to take a ride on the thing but all she could see was Paul and Gladys laughing and cooing on one another as though they were the only two people at the fair.

Paul stood on the merry-go-round platform as it spun around with his hand on Gladys' waist, while she was crying out like she was some kind of a child: "Paul, don't let go, don't let go!" as if the horse was doing anything but rising off the ground a foot or two. About a dozen children were riding on the thing all by themselves and here Gladys was nearly on the verge of hysterics. Clara just stared at the young woman, shaking her head and saying, "I think I'm going to be sick."

LONDON, ENGLAND–ENGLISH MANOR HOUSE BALCONY, EVENING 1694

On a second-floor balcony of the seventeenth century English manor, Lord Clemson/Paul Gabriel and his Lady Katherine/Gladys Hooper were embracing. The sounds of music from the ballroom below filtered up to where they were standing. Moonlight cascaded upon the two as Lord Clemson repeatedly kissed the woman's neck and face. Although she made a half-hearted attempt to push him away, Lady Katherine let him continue far longer than was appropriate for a woman of her station. The sensation of his lips caused her to lean her head back, exposing even more of her tender skin. Lord Clemson took it eagerly in his lips.

Ever so gently, Lady Katherine pushed him away, "Stop . . . I cannot."

"A man has desires," came the reply, as he continued to kiss her.

"I cannot . . . ," she said almost too softly, "please . . . stop."

Lord Clemson continued to kiss her, and she continued to allow herself to be kissed. A moment later, however, as Lord Clemson moved his hands to begin undoing the front of her dress, she pulled back angrily and slapped his face.

"No!" Lady Katherine replied angrily. "Not until after the wedding." Visibly upset, she began to cry and raced from the balcony toward a large room and out into the hallway beyond.

"Bloody 'ell," was all that passed through his lips, though the desire continued to well up within him. Realizing the best course of action was to follow after her and claim he had forgotten proper conduct in the presence of such beauty, he headed toward the hallway. At that moment, the silhouette of Betsy/Clara passed in front of the hallway door.

"Who be ye?" Lord Clemson asked, as he noticed she was carrying a tray with dishes toward the servant stairs.

The woman came to a stop, but said nothing.

"I say, who be ye?"

The voice cracked with surprise, "M' Lord?"

"Come hither."

The woman lowered her tray to a table before moving toward him. She wiped her hands on her apron and came toward the moonlight. As the light struck her face, Lord Clemson smiled and she curtsied.

"Do you have a name?" he inquired.

"Yes, m' Lord. Me name be Betsy."

He looked her over approvingly, for he had not realized he had such an attractive servant in his employ. "What are you doing?"

"The upstairs maid got a bit 'a fever, m' Lord. The head cook, Miz Wheeler, asked me to make 'er rounds."

Lord Clemson nodded with approval.

"I usually works in the kitchen, m' Lord." Clara added.

"I can see that." Lord Clemson reached out and touched the apron she was wearing, fingering the material between his hands. "It's certainly a bit of luck to find you here . . . I could use a little help from a woman, just now." His hands briefly brushed up against her breasts.

"I beg your pardon, m' Lord?"

"I could use a woman's help, just now."

Betsy was totally confused. "If you say so m' Lord."

"Oh, I say so." Lord Clemson raised a hand and began caressing the side of her face. "Betsy, it will be a sovereign for your troubles . . . and our little secret it will be." He moved his other hand around to her back and began untying her apron.

She froze with fear and confusion, "I don't understand m' Lord."

Lord Clemson only smiled, "Never been wenching . . . this is a bit 'a luck." He bent over and kissed her with an open mouth. She was so startled that she stood there and felt his lips grab hold of hers. He pulled her toward him and began kissing her on the neck, picking up where he had left off with Lady Katherine. The look on Betsy's face made it apparent that she was totally shocked by what was occurring.

Lord Clemson began to fondle her breast through her clothes with one hand, and with the other began to pull her dress up to where he could get to her undergarments.

"M' Lord?" Betsy's voice trembled with fear.

"Just relax," came the reply. "This is what all good servants do for their masters." His kisses became more forceful as he lowered her down to the floor. Her lips began to shake and her voice quivered with another, "M' Lord," as she felt his warm hand touch a part of her that no one had ever touched before. Lord Clemson was readying himself to disrobe when he heard footsteps coming down the hallway.

Suddenly, he jumped to his feet, pulling Betsy upright as well, and pushing her clothes back in place just as Lady Katherine's voice cried out, "Henry!" as the scene before her looked quite questionable.

Lord Clemson feigned a laugh and turned to his betrothed, "I knew you'd be watching, my love."

Suddenly, he swatted the scullery maid on the backside and spoke loud enough for his fiancée to hear. "Now, be off with ye."

"Yes, m' Lord," was all that she could say.

Betsy looked at him with eyes opened wide, looked toward Lady Katherine with fear, curtsied to them both and then scurried quickly from the room–stopping only long enough to retrieve the tray.

Lord Clemson reached out to Lady Katherine and smiled. "Won't you stand upon the balcony with me, m' dear? The moonlight is ever so lovely this time of night."

LONDON, ENGLAND–ENGLISH MANOR HOUSE KITCHEN, 1694

The Head Cook/Emily stared silently at Betsy/Clara, who appeared to be daydreaming yet again in the midst of scrubbing a pot. The Head Cook tapped a wooden spoon against the side of her hip, but still Betsy remained oblivious to the fact that she was being watched. Some of the other kitchen help began to snicker and laugh, and still Betsy appeared to be in another world daydreaming. One of the other maids, however, looked at Betsy sympathetically. (She would return as a sympathetic farmer's wife during the Fort Laramie period and again later, in the twentieth century, as Clara's sister-in-law, Nancy.)

Finally, Head Cook had had enough. She took her wooden spoon and slapped it down hard on the counter next to where Betsy had been working.

"What?!! I beg your pardon, mum." Betsy was completely startled.

"'ave ye gone completely daft?"

"No, mum."

"Will it be takin' ye a fortnight to wash the pans from now on?" The Head Cook asked angrily, pointing at the one pot the younger woman had been continually scrubbing.

"No, mum."

The older woman continued to shake the spoon as

she spoke: "Then, what in bloomin' 'ell is wrong with ye tonight?"

Betsy blushed with embarrassment. "Nothing, mum . . . nothing."

The Head Cook was unconvinced. "What is it?"

"Er . . . , not to worry yourself, mum."

"I be hearin' it now, or ye be on your way to another cook's kitchen, ye will."

Betsy pleaded, "Oh, no, mum. Don't put me out, mum."

The Head Cook waited impatiently until, finally, Betsy nodded her head in the direction of the ballroom. She answered nervously, "It's jus' that one of them kissed me tonight, mum."

All activity in the kitchen stopped and every servant turned to listen. The Head Cook was surprised, "Which one?"

"Lord Clemson, hisself, mum," came a soft reply.

The older woman was startled and disbelieving. "Lord Clemson . . . Lord Clemson been kissin' the likes of you." As she spoke the words aloud, the Head Cook began to laugh. She turned to the rest of the kitchen staff and made the announcement: "Did ye 'ear? Her ladyship 'ere's been kissin' Lord Clemson."

The staff began to laugh and jaunt, as well, and the Head Cook feigned a curtsy to the young woman and added: "I do hope the evening was sat'sfactory to you, mum. I hope you had time to enjoy ye'self, what between kissin' Lord Clemson and all . . . "

Tears rolled down Betsy's face as she began to cry. In exasperation, the head cook threw her wooden spoon in the pile with the rest of the pots and pans that Betsy was supposed to be washing. "Get back to ye washin' or I'll be done with ye."

The rest of the kitchen staff continued to laugh and snicker, while Betsy tried desperately to hold back her sobs.

SAMARIA CITY, IDAHO—STUART FAMILY HOME, EVENING, 1934

It was early morning, and thirteen-year-old Clara was sitting on the edge of her bed, day-dreaming. Emily's bed on the other side of the room was made, with Annabelle placed prominently against the headboard. Because Clara remained in her own little world, she remained oblivious to the fact that the bedroom door opened and sixteen-year-old Emily walked inside. Emily carried a stack of schoolbooks that she placed on the dresser. She turned to her sister, who had still not noticed her presence, and was obviously disgusted.

When it became clear that Clara remained in her own little world, Emily lifted the books about two feet off the dresser and let them drop back down hard.

Clara was completely startled. "What?!! Oh, I'm sorry . . . I was just thinking."

"Have you lost your mind?"

The Reincarnation of Clara

"No! I haven't lost my mind!"

"You're thinking about Paul again, weren't you?" Emily words were spoken with obvious distaste.

"Maybe." Was all the younger sister would say.

"Well, don't waste your time."

"Why not?"

"I can think of three very good reasons." Emily touched one finger after another on her left hand with each reason as she counted them off. "One—you're too young to date. Two—he's never gonna ask you out . . . not in a hundred years."

Clara made a face.

"And three—even if you were old enough, Mama and Papa will never let you!"

"We will see." Clara's words were spoken with more self-certainty than usual, causing Emily to watch her sister suspiciously, as if the younger girl knew something she wasn't saying.

Suddenly, there was a knock on the bedroom door, and it was Clara who spoke: "Come in, Jason."

Eighteen-year-old Jason opened the door wearing slacks and an undershirt. In his hands he held a dress shirt. He grinned.

"Clara, would you mind ironing my shirt? I got a date."

"So what's new about that?" Clara asked matter-of-factly, but she got up and took Jason's shirt nonetheless.

HUNTSVILLE, UTAH—SUMMER. LATE AFTERNOON, 2006

"I just loved your father, Jason." Eighty-five-year-old Clara remembered aloud. "He was always so enthusiastic about everything. Whenever you were around Jason, you were bound to have fun. After he and your mother, Nancy, moved down to Roy and he got a job there at Clearfield Auto Parts, Joe and I used to see them pretty regularly. It was a lot of fun for us. Your mother and I were more like sisters. We could talk about anything." Clara eyed the younger woman closely, "Nancy was the sister I never had."

"I remember." Joanie spoke softly.

"How long have your folks been gone?" Clara stopped rocking and looked sympathetically toward her niece.

"Dad died in '97, just before his eighty-first birthday. Mom's been gone for almost three years now."

Clara nodded, and continued to reflect aloud. "We loved the movies and driving up Ogden Canyon for dinner. There were a number of things we use to do pretty regularly. I remember the four of us always went to Ogden's Pioneer Day parade as an annual event. Sometimes we'd have another couple with us, and sometimes you kids would be there. You know how the Mormons love to treat July 24 as something pretty special." Clara smiled and looked up to make sure that Joanie was still writing. "Your Uncle Joe use to say that it was the biggest day of the year, second only to the birth of Christ. The day Brigham Young brought those Mormon pioneers into the valley."

"And said, 'this is the place,'" Joanie interrupted.

"That's right . . . that's right. Anyway, we use to find a place to stand right there on Washington Boulevard across from some motel and just watch that parade go by. Oftentimes we'd bring a few folding chairs and set them right there . . . I can't remember the name of the motel; it's gone now."

"It was the Travelodge."

"You remember?"

"I remember."

"I use to love that parade—the way they dressed up as pioneers, and all the wagons and clowns and horses. It was really something. Jason always had something positive to say about every outing we did together, and the parade was no exception. I remember once it had rained so hard that they postponed the thing for over an hour and we were just soppen wet, in spite of our umbrellas. That day the floats and the marching bands seemed to go by almost double-time just to get out of the weather. It was so bad that the makeup on some of the clowns had nearly run off. When the parade was over, walking back to the car, Jason said, 'the nice thing about today was the crowds was so thin that we didn't have a hard time seeing the parade . . . ,' and he was dead serious!" Clara chuckled.

"After Joe and your momma and dad had all died, I went by myself one year but I felt so lonely I had to leave before the first float even went by. It just wasn't the same. I ended up going to the mall just to keep from feeling sorry for myself."

"Sometimes there doesn't seem to be a choice to do much of anything else." Joan's words were spoken more for herself than for her aunt.

"It may seem that way, Joanie, but unfortunately when you feel sorry for yourself, it's often harder to see clear to what you're supposed to be doing about something."

"What do you mean?"

"I think that the one thing that blinds us to our own intuition the most, and the guidance right there in front of us, is our feelings and worries and hopes and dreams. All these emotions crowd in and make it harder to see your way clear."

"Are you saying that you could have seen a problem with Paul before it ever happened?"

"I did see a problem before it happened." Clara said positively. "Well, I nearly saw it. I started to see it on my wedding day, and I didn't want to see it."

"Are you serious? On your wedding day?"

Clara tapped the tabletop to add emphasis to her words. "On my wedding day."

SAMARIA CITY, IDAHO—BAPTIST CHURCH, FALL, 1940

The end of every pew and all the aisles of Samaria City's Baptist Church was decorated with flowers. Most of the guests had already arrived and taken their seats. The organist was softly playing her music, while the guests conversed quietly between themselves. Quite a few mentioned the fact that they never thought they'd see the day when Paul Gabriel would take a wife (especially not as early as twenty-two), as he seemed like the type who wanted to sow his oats.

Twenty-four-year-old Jason and twenty-five-year old Benjamin stood at the front of the church with Paul; both Jason and Benjamin were wearing their military uniforms. Off to one side of the church vestibule, a small dressing room held nineteen-year-old Clara, her sister, Emily, and Everett and Mabel Stuart. Emily waited patiently as Mabel looked over Clara's dress one last time, nodding her head with approval.

"You're absolutely beautiful, Clara."

"Thank you, Mama."

Everett Stuart toyed with the buttons of his shirt before turning to his wife. "Ma, are you sure this shirt looks okay?"

"Oh Everett, no one is even going to notice the bride's father."

Clara tried to sound reassuring: "You look great, Papa."

Finally, Emily spoke: "I never thought my little sister would get married before I did. And to Paul Gabriel, of all people."

"I told you he'd ask me out."

Emily just shrugged. "Now, that you caught him, I hope you know what to do with him."

Mabel Stuart spoke next. "Well, as long as this is what you want, Clara."

"Oh, it is Mama . . . I've wanted Paul for a million years. We're gonna be very happy . . . and I'm going to make you and Papa grandparents . . . "

"Don't talk about such things in the house of the Lord!" Mabel was horrified.

"Oh, Mama . . . the Lord knows all about sex."

Everett came next. "Just don't rush anything, Clara. Take some time to get to know Paul first."

"The rest of the girls in Samaria are way ahead of you on that one." Emily volunteered.

Clara gave her sister a disgusted look as Mabel spoke up: "Emily!"

"I'm sorry; I wish you both luck." Emily stated half-heartedly and then added: "Come on, Mama, we need to take our seats." Mabel nodded, gave Clara once last kiss on the check and said, "Just be happy," before following Emily into the church.

"It's not too late to change your mind." Everett volunteered when he was left alone with his daughter.

"Oh, Papa, this is what I want."

"Sometimes a package looks better before you open it."

The Reincarnation of Clara

"Don't worry, I'll be fine. I'm going to be a great wife and mother, you'll see."

Everett smiled. "Okay, just remember you were my daughter before you were his wife." Clara kissed her father on the cheek just as the organist began to play "Here Comes the Bride." Everett offered his daughter his arm, and the two of them entered the vestibule. With the start of the song, everyone in attendance stood up and watched.

In the first few rows near the front, on the groom's side of the seating arrangement, members of Paul's family appeared a little disheveled, but everyone was on their best behavior. Paul stood at the front of the church waiting for his bride. She smiled, and he smiled in return.

Suddenly, Clara was started to see the figure of her deceased grandfather standing halfway between her and Paul Gabriel. Although she smiled at him, and nodded, Grandpa Stuart appeared very stern and gloomy. Clara wondered what was wrong and as she looked back at Paul, his face seemed to change and suddenly became transformed. All at once Clara saw anger, hatred, abuse, control and rage on the face of the man she thought she loved. She looked back toward her grandfather, who said nothing but nodded with confirmation.

At first, a look of confusion began to cover Clara's face but she remembered where she was, what she was doing, and how long she had waited for this day.

She shook her head, brushed aside what she had just seen and looked back at Paul to see him appearing calm and collected.

When Clara turned to see her grandfather, he was gone.

NINE

HUNTSVILLE, UTAH—
SUMMER, LATE AFTERNOON, 2006

Joanie asked the question, "Do you know if your grandfather could look sideways?"

"He never discussed it, and by the time I was old enough to understand, he had already died. But one's talents remain a part of the soul for all time. So often while I was growing up, Grandpa Stuart seemed like he was keeping a big secret to himself. For that reason, one day I decided to look sideways at the question myself."

"Tell me what happened?"

"Well, Joanie, it doesn't have much to do with my time here in Huntsville."

"Please tell me Aunt Clara."

The old woman nodded, and started by saying: "Well, after I saw the flash of light, I found myself in a place and a time that I had never, ever been before . . . "

MOUNT CASIUS SETTLEMENT (ON THE BANKS OF THE MEDITERRANEAN BETWEEN MIZRAIM [ANCIENT EGYPT] AND CANAAN), EVENING, 1062 BC

It was evening and the moonlight shimmered upon the unusually smooth surface of the Mediterranean Sea. Near the shoreline, not far from the water's edge, a small encampment of nomads prepared for their evening meal. Desert children laughed and ran in between the tents, while men sat upon the ground and drank strong-smelling brew from leather pouches.

Women and young girls appeared to be doing all the work while their men folk sat idle. One of the elderly women shook her head in irritation as she looked over to her husband, who was already on the verge of passing out. Nearby, a goat was being roasted over an open flame, while some of the women were setting out crocks of dates and leeks and baskets of unleavened bread. Off to one side, three camels appeared content as the animals simply chewed a meal consisting of blades of grass and straw.

Off to one side, an invisible outline of forty-something Clara Cabot watched the scene with interest before seeing another burst of light.

MOUNTAIN CAVE ABOVE MEDITERRANEAN SHORELINE — SAME EVENING, 1062 BC

Quite suddenly, forty-something Clara Cabot found herself higher up the mountainside watching another scene from within the confines and safety of a cave. She nodded with approval, for at least here she recognized those who sat before her.

A small fire illuminated a darkened cave, causing shadows to dance upon the stone walls. An old bearded man, whom they called Ephraim (and whom Clara recognized as her present-day grandfather), looked proudly upon his nine-year-old daughter, Naomi (a girl, Clara recognized, as a nine-year-old version of herself). Naomi's haircut and attire appeared to be more like that of a boy's.

The inside of the cave was also illuminated by candlelight and the floor was lined with worn, woven, carpets. Assorted symbols, crystals, and runes were also scattered throughout, but the remaining furnishings were meager. The old man and his daughter sat cross-legged on the floor of the cave. Ephraim was talking while his daughter stared intently into the flame of the largest candle. Another twelve-year-old girl, stood quietly in the shadows fixing a meal with her mother. The girls name at the time had been Rachel, but Clara Cabot had no doubt that she was staring at an earlier version of Emily.

"There's always been Emily," Clara muttered to herself.

At first, the old man spoke in a mixture of Hebrew and Aramaic; however, as Clara listened with her mind, she began to hear English, with a Mediterranean accent:

"Focus . . . focus . . . ," came Ephraim's words. "Use the power of your mind."

Naomi remained still, staring silently into the candle flame. After another moment, the young girl saw a tremendous flash of light.

MOUNT CASIUS SETTLEMENT, SAME EVENING, 1062 BC

All at once, the scene that Clara Cabot had just visited appeared before the eyes of nine-year-old Naomi. Moonlight shimmered upon the smooth surface of the Mediterranean Sea. A small encampment of desert nomads prepared their evening meal near the shoreline. Children laughed and ran between tents, while men sat upon the ground and drank from leather pouches. Women and young girls continued working while the males remained idle. An elderly woman shook her head in irritation at the site of her husband's drunkenness. Even in the midst of the vision, Naomi could hear the voice of her father: "Now, what do you see?"

"I see a camp with many tents . . . and camels . . . a group of women are preparing a meal for their families."

"Good . . . good . . . And what do they eat?"

Naomi continued: "A goat is being roasted over an open flame. Some women are putting out crocks of dates and leeks, and baskets of unleavened bread. Off to one side, three camels appear content chewing a cud . . .

"I see bread, and honey, and olives, and dates . . . there is wine . . . " In Naomi's vision, several of the bearded tribesmen laughed and passed a clay flask between themselves.

Ephraim looked proudly at his daughter and nodded approvingly. "Now, imagine you have returned your mind to the candle . . . Focus . . . focus . . . focus . . . and you will find you have returned . . . here, in the cave, with your father, Ephraim . . . and when you have returned, you may open your eyes . . . "

The old man watched his daughter follow the instructions until she opened her eyes. When she had finished, he reached out and touched the side of her face. "You learn quickly, my child. Not everyone is such a good student."

Twelve-year-old Rachel frowned at her father's words, but continued working. The old man appeared oblivious to his eldest daughter and reached out again, stroking the side of his youngest child's face.

"Better even than a boy?"

The old man smiled again. "Better than a boy."

"That was fun! How did I do it?"

"In the same manner that your mind wanders in dreams while you sleep. You see my child, the body does not limit the mind."

"Can I do it again?"

Ephraim sighed and looked to see that his wife and eldest daughter had finished preparing the meal. "It grows late . . . we will try again tomorrow."

Although disappointed, Naomi agreed but asked, "Father, will I always be able to do it . . . even when I'm old like you?"

He was amused. "If you practice it will become a part of who you are. If you work at it, you will remember always . . . "

"Always?"

"Always!" The old man appeared serious, but his nod was one of complete certainty.

HUNTSVILLE, UTAH—SUMMER, LATE AFTERNOON, 2006

After returning from the "little girl's room," as she continued to call it, even at the age of eighty-five, Clara Cabot walked around the hatbox next to her rocker, and reached for a drink from her glass, before finally sitting back down. On top of the table, Joanie was sorting through a stack of digital tapes lying next to her writing tablet. The younger woman pointed in the direction of her notes and the tape recorder.

"This is much different that I was expecting."

Clara chuckled. "I don't know if the Tribune will be getting their money's worth—we've skipped all over Huntsville and back."

"Oh, I've got plenty here for that, but the rest of it, well, it just makes everything seem like its part of a larger purpose."

Clara leaned in the direction of her niece. "Quite a system the good Lord set up, isn't it?" The roaring sounds of a jet engine flew overhead, and Clara shook her head with irritation. "Just like the old days . . . I thought we were done with that."

HUNTSVILLE, UTAH—CLARA'S VICTORIAN PORCH, 1964

Forty-seven-year-old Joe Cabot pointed out the type of jet flying overhead to his forty-eight-year-old brother-in-law, Jason Stuart, as the two walked down the porch steps in the direction of the perimeter fence. Forty-three-year-old Clara Cabot sat on the porch with Nancy, thirty-eight and noticeably pregnant. Nancy's purse sat on the table beside her.

Nancy glanced in the direction of her husband and Joe. When it appeared safe, she pulled a copy of the book *Many Mansions* out of her bag.

"Thanks for the book, Clara. Jason says reincarnation is nothing but foolishness but I couldn't put it down. Do you think I lived before?"

"We've all lived before," Clara chuckled, "even Jason."

"Could you tell me something about *my* past?"

"What would you like to know?" and then she added, "Let me hold onto your watch."

Nancy looked at her inquisitively as Clara extended her palm. "Everything you wear contains the vibrations of who you are. If I hold your watch, it's easier to tune in."

The sound of another jet engine roared past and Clara was obviously irritated. Nonetheless, she took Nancy's watch and took a deep breath. She began staring at her sister-in-law until there was a tremendous flash of light, just as Nancy asked, "Did we know each other before?"

FORT LARAMIE, WYOMING—FORT ENCLOSURE, NOVEMBER, 1852

Esther/Clara walked through the street out in front of the saloon, carrying her baby girl in the direction of the chapel. As she walked, Esther passed in front of the transparent form of her 1964 self, standing off to one side as an observer. Esther's steps were obviously quite determined.

Reverend Vaux/Everett Stuart stood out in front of the chapel watching the children in his care playing nearby. He grimaced as he saw Esther's approach.

"What do you want?"

"Reverend . . . I need someone to look after my baby." Esther lowered the child toward him so that he could see the baby's face. However, Reverend Vaux was repulsed.

"I don't want no bastard child cursin' the ground of a good Christian school. Take it away."

Esther sighed. "I'm leaving soon and my baby needs a home. She needs to be with someone who can care for her . . . she needs to be with other children."

"Find one of your own to take it . . . ," he said, waving her aside.

"But reverend, she's just a baby."

"I said take it away." Reverend Vaux turned away and started walking toward the chapel. Esther looked down at her child and shook her head in disappointment.

"Don't worry, I'll find someone to take care of you."

She turned and headed down the dirt-lined street, looking for anyone who could take her daughter. She next came to a farmer and his wife, but after explaining what she wanted the couple shook their heads and continued walking even faster on their way. In front of the blacksmith's, Esther ran into an old woman. She showed the baby and pleaded with the woman to take the child, but the old woman touched the wrinkles on her own face and hands, as she explained that she was far too advanced in years for such a young child. Repeatedly, Esther was disappointed in her quest.

Although several couples passed Esther on their way to the hotel or to and from the stables, no one was willing to accept the baby. Finally, Esther returned to the saloon porch, tired and depressed, and attempted to pass the child to Mary/Mabel Stuart who was sympathetic.

"Oh. Esther, I would love this child, but the baby needs a real mother." Mary reached out and touched Esther on the shoulder, "Are you sure you and Russ can't give this baby a home?"

"I can't . . . we can't." Esther was adamant. "It just won't work.

Nearby, the invisible outline of 1964's Clara Cabot wiped a tear from her eyes, and whispered sadly, "You will live to regret this day."

After resting on the porch with Mary for a moment longer, Esther left the saloon and continued her search through Fort Laramie's encampment. Time and again, she explained what she wanted to a couple or to a woman walking by herself until her hair was disheveled, her eyes were glazed with tears, and she was exhausted. Finally, Esther approached a Sioux and his squaw and explained as best as she could with hand motions that she wanted to give the couple her child. Although the Indian woman briefly fingered the infant's blanket, she patted her own stomach to make it quite clear that she was already with child. Disappointed and exhausted, and not knowing what else to do, Esther turned to head back to the saloon. At that moment, a wagon came to a stop in the front of the hotel.

A young farmer drove the wagon with his wife seated next to him. The young man helped his wife down from her seat just as Esther approached. When the wife turned to look at Esther, 1964's Clara could see that the young wife was 1964's Nancy Stuart.

Esther explained what she wanted to the couple. The wife looked lovingly at the baby and then sympathetically at Esther. After gazing at the child for a moment longer, the younger woman extended her arms and took Esther's baby. She cuddled the child and cooed into its ear, while her husband looked on. Finally, the young woman turned to her husband as though pleading and, after a momentary hesitation, he smiled, and nodded with approval.

Esther smiled, touched the child one last time on the brow, turned, and walked away. A tear appeared in the corner of her eye, but she wiped it aside and headed back in the direction of the saloon.

HUNTSVILLE, UTAH—SUMMER, LATE AFTERNOON, 2006

Joan was stunned. Clara only smiled. Finally, it was Joanie who spoke: "Is that why you and Mama were so close?"

"Everyone with whom we have an emotional connection—good or bad—has been there before."

Joan looks at her inquisitively. "Everyone?"

Clara nodded. "Everyone! Although relationships change . . . We encounter no one by chance."

"And everyone comes back to us?"

"Yes, and everything we do comes back to us."

Joanie sighed. "Doesn't that mean we make the same mistakes over and over again?"

"God, I hope not . . . ," Clara chucked. "No, Joanie, there's always learning. At the core of our being, we're always learning—even from our mistakes. I paid dearly for giving up my child in Ft. Laramie. In fact, the same day your mother first asked me to look sideways for her, I saw just how much I had paid, and all the pieces finally came together . . . "

HUNTSVILLE, UTAH—CLARA'S VICTORIAN HOME, 1964

It was early afternoon and the two couples (Joe and Clara Cabot and Jason and Nancy Stuart) were sitting around the dining table, talking. They had just finished eating, and the empty plates in front of them had yet to be cleared. Jason turned to Joe:

"How about a cigarette?"

Nancy was quick to speak up: "Not around the baby! You'll have to go outside."

Jason smiled and rolled his eyes. "The baby is not

The Reincarnation of Clara

even here yet, and already I'm dealing with a new mother."

Jason got up from the table and turned to briefly kiss his wife. Joe rose, as well, and winked at Clara: "See you later, darlin'." With that, the two men headed out the front door.

Nancy waited until they were alone. "We didn't get a chance to finish. I want to know what else you can see?" Nancy took off her watch and passed it to Clara.

"Okay . . . I'll tell you, but I don't know how much you're ready to hear."

"Just tell me whatever you see."

A moment later, forty-three-year-old Clara saw a tremendous flash of light.

FORT LARAMIE, WYOMING—FORT ENCLOSURE, NOVEMBER, 1852

Mary/Mabel Stuart and Esther/Clara Cabot were standing out front of the saloon saying their good-byes. The two women embraced, obviously upset about the parting. It was Mary who spoke:

"Are you sure you're going to be okay about the baby?"

Esther was positive. "I'm fine. I *know* the baby will be just fine. Besides, if Russ and I want kids, we'll just have some more . . . "

"What about his leg?"

"Doc said he was lucky to be alive—he'll have a limp, but he should be good as new in no time."

Mary reflected aloud. "Maybe I should have taken the baby."

Esther chuckled. "You're worrying more about the baby than I am."

"I know, but I feel guilty. Maybe a daughter would have been the final push I needed to get me out of here."

All at once the saloon doors flung open and Russell/Joe Cabot limped outside and stepped unto the porch to join them. He walked with a cane and was obviously in quite a bit of pain.

Russ winked at Esther, "We'll darlin', you get your wish. We're off to Californy. Me and you together, at last."

The invisible form of 1964's Clara watched at the two women embraced and said their final good-byes.

Mary began to cry. "Promise we'll see each other again."

Esther was tearful. "I promise."

1964's Clara wiped a tear from her own eyes, just as she heard the voice of Nancy Stuart coming from a long ways away: "Can you see what happened to Esther's baby?"

The invisible woman answered, "Just a minute . . . I'm looking." And in the midst of Mary and Esther's final embrace on the saloon porch, there was a tremendous flash of light.

SAMARIA CITY, IDAHO—STUART FAMILY HOME, EVENING, 1928

The four Stuart children: Benjamin (at thirteen), Jason (at twelve), Emily (at ten), and Clara (at seven) were sitting around the kitchen table with Grandpa Stuart, who was smoking his pipe. Over and over again, the children took turns staring anxiously toward the closed door of their parents' bedroom.

"It will be any time now," Grandpa Stuart assured them.

Finally, the bedroom door opened and a midwife stepped aside so that Everett Stuart could carry the new child, baby Sara (cleaned and wrapped in a blanket), to meet her siblings. Everett Stuart brought the infant to the table and lowered it so that everyone could see.

Everett was obviously proud of the new delivery. "I want you all to meet baby Sara."

One at a time, he showed the baby to everyone around the table, beginning with Benjamin, then Jason, then Emily, and then Grandpa Stuart. When Clara's grandfather saw the child's face he smiled, and nodded with approval. While seven-year-old Clara looked at little Sara and touched her face, Grandpa Stuart spoke:

"You need to be especially nice to this child, Clara. You need to try and be the best big sister in the whole world to that little girl."

Clara was overjoyed. "Oh, I will Grandpa . . . I will. Can I hold her, Papa?"

Everett Stuart nodded and placed the tiny infant in Clara's outstretched arms. Emily frowned, because she had wanted to hold the baby first.

TEN

HUNTSVILLE, UTAH— SUMMER, LATE AFTERNOON, 2006

"Aunt Clara, why don't more of us remember?"

"Oh, in part we do remember—we have all got biasis and likes and dislikes. How often do we meet someone for the very first time and for some reason not like that person? Or how often do we meet someone and for no reason whatsoever, we're instant friends? Thank God, we don't have to deal with all of the individual pains and sorrows of more than one life at a time . . . but in a sense, we do remember, Joanie. Everything from the past has molded us into who we are right now." She paused and began chuckling. "You're very different from your brother, Jimmy, aren't you?"

Joanie rolled her eyes and shook her head in amazement, "Worlds apart!"

"And didn't you have the exact same upbringing?" Joanie nodded.

"You see, Joanie, we don't start off life as a clean slate. We pick up exactly were we left off."

"Can I ask you something, Aunt Clara?"

"Anything, Joanie, anything."

"You and I always seemed to have a hard time. Did we know each other before?"

Clara looked at her niece with love, nodded, and reached out to take her hand. "Child, we have known each other many, many times." With just a little difficulty, the old woman reached down and picked up the hatbox that had been sitting next to her rocking chair all through the day. She pushed the box over the table toward her niece. "I've been wanting to give this to you for a very long time."

"What is it?"

Clara only smiled. "Something that belongs to you."

Joanie lifted the lid off of the hatbox and peered inside. Lying on top of a pile of crushed tissue paper was a doll—beautiful but obviously old.

"Her name is Annabelle . . . "

"Aunt Emily's doll?" Joanie asked with surprise.

Clara nodded. "I've been holding onto it ever since she died."

Joan appeared stunned. "You think I'm Emily?"

"I have known since before you were even born.

Let me tell you a story, Joanie, after that I'm hoping we can be friends."

HUNTSVILLE, UTAH—CLARA'S VICTORIAN HOME, 1964

Clara Cabot and Nancy Stuart remained alone at the dining table. Clara's eyes remained glassy and fixated as Nancy asked another question: "Can you tell me about the baby? Jason's hoping for a boy."

The question prompted another flash of light.

ROY, UTAH –JASON AND NANCY STUART FAMILY HOME, JOAN STUART'S BEDROOM—1967

The invisible form of forty-something Clara Cabot watched as a two-year-old girl scurried happily over the grass between her mother and father, Nancy and Jason Stuart. It was obvious that Nancy Stuart was pregnant for a second time.

The invisible Clara spoke, knowing that 1964's Nancy could hear her words: "Not this time . . . You're going to have a girl."

From a long ways away, forty-something Clara Cabot heard the words: "What is she like?" And there was a flash of light.

ROY, UTAH –JASON AND NANCY STUART FAMILY HOME, JOAN STUART'S BEDROOM—1976

Invisible Clara Cabot found herself standing in the room of an eleven-year-old girl. The young girl was lying on her stomach in bed with a spiral notebook. She was writing, and it was clear that she had already written many pages. Her back was facing the forty-something form of Clara Cabot.

The invisible Clara spoke with certainty: "She'll be a writer."

From a long way away, Nancy Stuart asked, "Can you see anything else?"

Clara looked around the room. A mirror and dresser were against one wall, and a large brush sat on top of the dresser. Clara could see her own invisible reflection in the mirror. A moment later, the eleven year old got up from the bed and turned to look in the mirror. Clara gasped when she recognized that the child was an eleven-year-old version of her sister, Emily.

HUNTSVILLE, UTAH—SUMMER, LATE AFTERNOON, 2006

Joan was stunned. She sat in silence until Clara reached out to take her hand:

"Are you okay?" the old woman asked.

"I *was* Emily." Joanie sighed.

Clara nodded.

"Is it possible for us to start over?" Joanie asked.

"Yes, in fact, I want you to come here and live with me. It will be good for when the baby's born. I'd like to help you. It will also be a wonderful way for us to get to know each other."

Joanie appeared surprised by the offer.

"What did mom think when you first told her this story?"

Clara chuckled. "What's your middle name . . . ?"

"Emily?"

"It seems to me that she took it pretty well."

"This whole thing is just so . . . so incredible. "

"Each of us is like an archaeological dig. Every layer we scratch away leads to a whole new story. I'm glad we finally had the opportunity to talk, Joanie, we've wasted too much time already."

Joanie smiled at her aunt. "I think I would like to come here, Aunt Clara. It would be good for me and the baby, plus I'm certain you've got a lot more stories you could tell me."

"You have no idea." Clara chuckled.

Joanie nodded, and then began removing her watch. "Aunt Clara, can you tell me about my baby?"

Clara waved the watch aside. "I'd be delighted. But I don't need that."

Joanie looked at her with confusion.

"I've had a lot more practice."

Clara smiled, took a deep breath and began focusing on her niece. Suddenly, there was a tremendous flash of light.

SAMARIA CITY, IDAHO—STUART FAMILY HOME, 1932

Eighty-five-year-old Clara found herself standing in the yard of her childhood home. From off in the distance she could hear Joan repeat her words: "What can you tell me about the baby?"

All at once, Clara saw four-year-old Sara Stuart appear next to the duck enclosure, surrounding by clouds and light. Sara looked up, smiled and waved.

The old woman looked at the young child inquisitively, and Sara nodded.

Joanie's words came from a very long ways away: "What do you see?"

Eighty-five-year-old Clara Cabot smiled and began to cry with joy, "Something truly wonderful . . . "

Made in the USA
Columbia, SC
05 March 2020